MASTERS OF THE GAME

COBRA

MASTERS OF THE GAME

COBRA

BRENDA JACKSON

LOVE, PASSION AND PROMISE BOOKS
are published by
The Madaris Publishing Company
P O Box 28267
Jacksonville, FL 32226

ISBN - 979-8-9932569-2-4
10 9 8 7 6 5 4 3 2 1
Printed in the United States of America

Love, Passion and Promise
An Imprint of the Madaris Publishing Company
www.madarispublishing.com

BOOKS IN THE BENNETTS
AND MASTERS FAMILY SERIES
BY BRENDA JACKSON

A Family Reunion
The Savvy Sistahs
The Sweetest Taboo
What a Woman Wants
Her Little Black Book
The Bennetts' Wedding
The Bennetts' Christmas
Masters of the Game – Colton
Masters of the Game – Cobra

DEDICATION

To my husband, Gerald Jackson, Sr. - You are the best thing that has ever happened to me, and you will forever be in my heart.

To everyone who believes in the power of true love.

To my readers who enjoy the Masters and Bennett families.

To my sons – Gerald Jackson, Jr. and Brandon. You are my heartbeats.

"And Jesus answered and said unto them,
Take heed that no man deceive you."
– Matthew 24:4 KJV

CHAPTER 1

The moment the woman walked into Swanky's, wearing a tight-ass dress with a split nearly to her waist, Cobra Masters had known that the night would end with him in her bed, or her in his. Her name was Allison, and she'd explained that they'd have to go to his place, since she had two small kids at home with a babysitter.

No problem. They had left her car at the nightclub, and on the drive over, he had explained his expectations and rules. All they would have was one night. He didn't do sleepovers. Nor did he do repeats. No exceptions. She expressed her understanding while keeping her hand firmly planted on his crotch as he drove. He couldn't wait to get her into bed.

She made some admiring comments about his house as he drove up the long-winding driveway, and he accepted her compliments in stride. There was no need to tell her this was not his primary home. He lived in New York and was only in Savannah on a short visit. Nor did she need to know that he was part of a set of triplets, and that all three brothers owned second homes in the town where they had been born and raised.

A ton of Masters lived in Savannah. And Cobra had friends who still lived here. Sheriff Liam Strawberry had been his best friend since forever, and Titus Gaffney, the newly elected mayor, was his best friend from college at Harvard.

But the only thing Allison needed to know was the rules he'd told her, and he'd deliver a night she wouldn't forget.

He'd barely turned off his alarm system and hustled her inside his house before she began removing her clothes. Then she raced upstairs—naked—after snatching the bottle of wine and two glasses off his counter. He followed her, loving her energy and ready for the fun to begin. He hadn't felt this playful in years. Damn, she was beautiful naked, and he couldn't wait to get inside of her.

While she poured two glasses of wine and set them on the nightstand, he stripped down to his boxers...then remembered something. He let out an expletive.

She was already in his bed, legs spread wide. Propping up on the pillow to look at him, she asked, "What's wrong?"

"I forgot to do something downstairs." He absently tossed the condom pack he'd taken out of his pants on the nightstand near the wine glasses. "Stay in that position, Allison. I'll be right back."

Rushing down the stairs, he went into his office, where a good friend from high school, Anthony Tombstone, had installed state-of-the-art video cameras around his property and in every room of his house. Tombstone owned a security company, and the last thing Cobra wanted was for anyone— including his friend—to see video footage of what was about to go down in his bedroom.

He was about to switch off that particular monitor when he saw Allison slide off the bed. Hadn't he told her to stay where she was? His greedy eyes were glued to her naked ass, so he almost didn't notice her quickly pulling a miniature packet from the wide-band gold bracelet around her wrist. Looking over her shoulder to make sure he wasn't coming back into the room, she quickly emptied the contents into one of the wine glasses.

What the hell! She was spiking his drink! If that wasn't bad enough, she then pulled a decorative hairpin from her hair and began using it to poke holes in the condom pack, destroying at least half a dozen of them.

His arousal was now replaced by fury. Picking up his office landline, he pushed a button. Seconds later, a male voice said, "Cobra, I heard you were in town."

"Tombstone, I need you to permanently save tonight's video footage. Inside and outside. Especially, from my bedroom. I came into my office to disconnect the camera in my bedroom and saw the woman I'd left upstairs not only spiking my wine but also poking holes in my condom packs."

"Damn! It's a good thing you saw her—and got a recording of it. You need to file charges against her ass. Have her arrested. Poking holes in condoms is considered a form of sexual assault, and there's no telling what she put in your drink."

"You better believe I will be pressing charges," Cobra said. "Contact Straw. Send him here immediately."

"Will do. I know for a fact he's on duty tonight."

"Good," Cobra said.

"In the meantime, make sure she doesn't try to get rid of the evidence. And I know just how to make sure that she doesn't."

"How?" Cobra asked, almost too afraid to know. In high school, Tombstone was the class prankster.

"Listen up, Masters."

Moments later, Cobra rushed back up the stairs. Allison appeared to be in the same spot he'd left her. Quickly grabbing his pants off the floor, he stared at her. Seeing her legs open wide in invitation was suddenly a total turn-off. "Get up! We need to get out of here and hide in my basement."

"What!" she shrieked, closing her legs. "Hide in your basement? Why?" she asked, getting off the bed.

"A few guys from my gang found out I ratted on them. I just got word from my homies that they're on their way to kill me, and anyone I'm with. Execution style."

"Jesus!" she said, "I need to leave here now."

He heard the panic in her voice. "You can't leave. They already have this place surrounded. They will blow your head off the minute you open the front door. Since I parked in the garage and the lights are still off downstairs, they don't know for certain that I'm home."

"What about the light in here?"

"The window in this room faces the backyard, they probably can't see it. We need to hide out in my basement until I'm sure they are gone. Hurry up. Your clothes are downstairs. Grab them off the floor. You can dress in the basement. There's a light down there."

Her naked ass rushed past him, literally running down the stairs at breakneck speed. He had put on his pants and slid into his shirt by the time he joined her. She had managed to slide into that tight-ass dress in the dark, but carried her shoes in her hand.

"Come on," he whispered.

"Shouldn't you call the police?" she whispered back.

"I already have. But there's no telling how long it might take them to get here. They know the kind of business I'm in and probably wouldn't be too sad if I got my head blown off."

"Mercy!"

He opened the door that led to the basement. "One of my homies will alert me when the danger has passed."

"I have two kids at home who need me," she wailed, seemingly on the verge of a panic attack. "I would never have come here with you tonight had I known you were a gangsta. I assumed you were some high-class businessman."

"Please keep your voice down if you want us to get out of here alive," he warned, not wanting to hear anything she had to say.

She glared at him, but did lower her voice. "I should have known you were a liar when you claimed your name was Cobra. No sane mother would name her kid that. When this is over, I hope I never see you again."

He had news for her: he *would* be seeing her again. In court. He would make sure they locked her up and threw away the key. Instead of responding to her continued tirade, he remained quiet and kept his cool.

A short while later, his Apple watch dinged.

"What was that?" she asked, standing close behind him.

"An alert to let me know the police have arrived."

"Praise Him!" Allison said, almost dropping to her knees in thanks. "The sooner I leave here, the better."

Cobra opened the basement door, and she swept past him. Just then, he heard his name being called from the living room. Recognizing the voice, he said, "In the kitchen, Straw."

The kitchen lights came on and three police officers entered. Liam Strawberry had been given the nickname Straw in elementary school, a shortened version of his last name and a reference to his physique—he was tall and lanky. He'd played basketball in college until a knee injury had ended what everyone had assumed would be a promising NBA career.

"I was on the other side of town, but I got here as fast as I could. Tombstone told me what was going down, and some of my men are collecting the evidence. By the way, Tomb sent over a copy of the video."

"Good."

"Look, officer," Allison was saying, "I need to call an Uber for a ride back to my car. I had no idea things would end up like this when I left Swanky's with this guy."

"I'm sure you didn't. And I'm not an officer. I'm the sheriff. Sheriff Strawberry."

She nodded. "Sheriff Strawberry, it's nice to meet you. But as I said, I need to go. I'm not the type of woman to associate with gangstas."

"Unfortunately, miss, the only place you're going is down to the station. You're under arrest."

Shock crossed her face when two officers approached her with handcuffs. "Under arrest?"

"Yes," Sheriff Strawberry said, not smiling. "And I'll need these for evidence," he said, removing her bracelet and the hairpin and slipping them into clear evidence bags.

"But I'm not the gangsta. He is," she said, pointing at Cobra. "And you have no right to take my belongings."

"Ma'am, you are under arrest for sexual assault."

"Sexual assault!" she exclaimed, nearly screaming the words at the top of her voice.

"Yes, tampering with a condom is a crime. As is spiking someone's wine."

A flash of guilt on her face was quickly replaced with fury. "Lies! You can't prove a thing."

Sheriff Strawberry chuckled. "Unfortunately, we can. You were caught on a video camera in his bedroom. And it can be backed up by evidence—the tampered condom packets, the drink, as well as this bracelet, which has a secret compartment. It shouldn't be too hard to prove that the holes in the condoms were made by that hairpin." He nodded to the two officers. "Put her in the squad car."

She turned and, with her hands cuffed, she struck out at Cobra, hitting his knee and thigh with her feet, while spewing obscenities. It was apparent she'd been aiming for his balls. The two officers finally got her under control.

Once she was safely in the back seat of a squad car, Cobra said, "Make sure you add assault and battery to the charges, Straw."

His best friend looked at him and shook his head. "One day you'll take my advice and put a lock on your zipper, Cobra. And you need to follow me to the precinct to give a statement."

"No problem. I'll call Tez to meet me there."

Straw lifted a brow. "So, the hot-shot attorney is in town, too?"

"Yes. All three of us are. The church is honoring Uncle Howey on Sunday, in an appreciation dinner, and we came home for that."

"That's right. Mom did mention something about a dinner at the banquet hall you and your brothers built for the church. And to think that the woman we arrested thinks you're a gangsta. You'd better hope Ms. Inez doesn't hear about this."

He hoped his mother didn't hear about it either. "There is no reason why she should. This was official police business, and I'm asking that it not be broadcast. Just make sure you don't let anything slip to your mother." Straw's mother, Molly Collins-Strawberry, and Inez Masters had been thick as thieves since high school.

"I'll make sure this doesn't get leaked to the press on our end, Cobra," Straw said.

"Thanks."

***

A few hours later, the triplets–Cortez, Colton, and Cobra —sat in Cobra's home nursing their favorite drink—scotch. Cortez was married and lived in LA with his wife, Victoria. Three months ago, they had welcomed their son, Cornell Masters, into the world. On the same day, Victoria's cousin, Kennedy, and her husband, Haddison, also gave birth to a son they named Bracen Maceo Wolf.

Colton was engaged to be married in June–seven months from now–to Kelly Perkins. Everybody was happy for Colton and Kelly and excited about their wedding plans. Kelly, who owned the KP Consulting Agency, had been brought on to work exclusively for Masters Unlimited and would be opening branch offices in Boston and New York.

It was a cold night in November, and the brothers appreciated the heat from the fireplace. And Cobra was enjoying the downtime with his brothers. His trip to the sheriff's office had lasted three hours, far longer than it should have. But Allison–whose real name had turned out to be Bernice Whey —had tried to retaliate against Cobra by claiming he had not mentioned there was a video camera in his bedroom and had invited her to his home for the sole purpose of taping their sexual activities. Her attorney, who showed up looking as if he'd slept in his suit for the last two days, immediately jumped on Bernice's allegations and suggested that Cobra drop the charges against his client.

Speaking on his brother—and client's—behalf, Attorney Cortez Masters outright refused the offer. He made it clear the charges would hold, and that if Bernice Whey, aka Allison, tried to drum up false allegations against his client, he had no problem taking it to trial. This wasn't the first time he'd come across a woman like Bernice. In fact, he'd seen several. And in his experience, it wasn't usually too difficult to prove the woman had a pattern of this sort of behavior with other men.

All it had taken was a call to Peachtree Investigations, where Landon Chestnut was a partner. Landon was a family member by marriage with Cortez, and a good friend of Colton's and Cobra's. Within an hour, Landon had uncovered damning documentation filed a few years earlier by both fathers of Bernice's two kids. The files stated that each man—who admitted having sex with her, and DNA backed up that the child in question was theirs—had used a condom. Given what he now knew about Bernice's methods, Cobra guessed that the condoms used back then had been tampered with as well. Only then, she hadn't been caught. This time, she had.

Cobra had been watching Bernice Whey the entire time, saw how nervous she'd become when Cortez started revealing what he had discovered about her in just a short period of time. He had a feeling there was more she didn't want to come out, especially now that she knew a private investigative firm was doing the digging.

In a surprising move, she pleaded guilty to all charges—two counts of sexual assault for the condom tampering and spiking of the wine, along with assault and battery. She was released on bond but had to return for sentencing in a month.

"You know, Straw might have a point, Cobra," his brother Colton said, breaking the silence. "You need to put a lock on your zipper."

"It's not a bad idea," Cortez added, grinning.

Cobra honestly didn't see anything amusing about the situation. What if he hadn't seen that video? What if he'd fallen prey to Bernice's plan? Hell, he had no doubt that in nine months, she would have been on his doorstep, claiming that he was her baby's daddy. And once it was proven true, he would have been responsible for a child he had been tricked into making.

And another thing. If Cortez hadn't forced the woman to drop her frivolous claim that he'd invited her to his house so he could video their bedroom activities, he could have been charged with a sexual offense. He didn't want to think about what would have tarnished his character and business reputation. Tonight's events had definitely been a wake-up call for him.

"I think you guys and Straw are right. I plan to take that advice."

His two brothers stared at him for a moment, and as if he needed clarification, Colton asked, "And that advice is…?"

"I'm keeping my zipper locked."

Now that got his brothers laughing. "What do the two of you find so funny?"

"There's no way in hell you can go without sex," Cortez said.

Cobra shrugged. "I don't see why not."

"Well, I can," Colton said. "For years, you've told anyone who would listen that regular sex keeps the mind sharp."

"And I still stand by that," Cobra confessed. "But regardless, I think I'll manage to survive going without sex for a year."

"A year!" Cortez and Colton exclaimed simultaneously. "No way you'll last a year," Colton said.

A smirk appeared on Cobra's face. "An all-expense-paid trip to the Bahamas for a week says I can."

"You're on," Colton said.

Cobra then looked at Cortez. "And I bet you four prepaid airline tickets–first class–anywhere in the country, over the course of a year, tickets I had planned to use for whenever I wanted to visit my favorite nephew in LA, that I will last without sex for a year."

Cortez smiled. "First of all, Cornell is your only nephew, and since you will lose, I have no problem going along with this."

"Neither of you will win the bet," Cobra said. "After what Bernice, Allison, or whatever her name was, tried tonight, I am through with women."

"For a year?" Colton asked.

"For longer than that, but for the bet, a year is good," Cobra said. "Even if I *am* attracted to someone, all I'll have to do is remember what went down tonight to kill my desire."

Cortez rolled his eyes. "We'll see. And you have to be honest with us, Cobra, if you fail and can't hold out for the year. Then we win."

"You guys won't win."

"Let's shake on the bet," Colton said.

The three brothers placed their glasses of Scotch aside, then held out their hands, shaking on their bet and sealing the deal.

CHAPTER 2

Seven months later

Cobra Masters took a sip of champagne and glanced around the huge ballroom of the St. Laurent Hotel-Atlanta. It had been just a year ago this month when he'd been in this same place, for the wedding reception of Landon Chestnut and Monica Bennett.

Today, his brother Colton had married Kelly. A few years ago, his brother Cortez had married Victoria. Cobra smiled, realizing that he was officially the last of the single Masters triplets. He was happy for Tez and Colt—they had married well. And it wasn't just that their wives' physical beauty was striking. He couldn't help but admire his sisters-in-law's other attributes.

They were both women who were selfless, confident, and not self-centered, women comfortable in their own skin, mature, and not drama queens. Women whose character was flawless; definite assets to the Masters family. They were exactly the type of woman he would marry...if he was interested in doing such a thing.

He wasn't.

Hell would freeze over first. He respected women, but wasn't ready to share his life with one. Women, in Cobra's opinion, were for pleasure. And he didn't feel bad thinking that way since he figured his place in their life was for the same reason. At least, that was the way it had been until an encounter with Bernice Whey had changed everything. And that one bad choice was the reason for his current hellish predicament, as well as that damn bet he'd made with his brothers that he wouldn't get laid for a year.

Granted, things had started off well, and resisting attractive women had been easy. A challenge, yes, but one he could handle.

However, the closer he got to the one-year mark, the harder he was finding it to keep that lock on his zipper. Temptation was a bitch. Especially on days like today, when he was surrounded by so many gorgeous women, with some of the most curvaceous bodies he had ever seen. Women always looked good at weddings, and today was no exception.

"You okay, Cobra?"

He glanced over at his brother Cortez. Both of them had been their brother's best men. Now things were winding down at the reception, and it wouldn't be long before the bride and groom took off. Then he could get the hell out of here and go to his hotel room alone, which would be a challenge in itself. After all, he had never attended a wedding where he hadn't taken some woman to bed afterwards.

"Why wouldn't I be?"

A smile shone on his brother's face while he sipped his champagne. "So, how long do you have to go now?"

That answer was easy. "Five months, one week, four hours, and..." he glanced at his watch, "thirty-three minutes."

Cortez chuckled. "Not surprised you're counting. Especially today, with so many beautiful women here. Of course, my wife is the most gorgeous one of them all."

"Of course," Cobra answered dryly.

"And of course, Victoria is off limits," Cortez said. "Although you wouldn't think so, the way Straw and Tomb are following her around, hanging on her every word."

Cobra hid his grin. He looked around and found Victoria holding court with their two childhood friends. Cortez saw them as well. But Cobra knew that his brother wasn't the least bit jealous. It was obvious to anyone looking that Straw and Tomb thought the world of Victoria, and had, ever since she had helped them out of a jam.

Two years ago, in the spring, she had come to Savannah with Cortez and had spent a lot of time sprucing up Straw and Tomb's mothers' yards with all kinds of plants and flowers—something the two moms had been asking their sons to do for years.

But it was more than that. Victoria, who owned a national landscaping company, had gone all out. That year, both yards had been featured in a national home-and-garden magazine. The same one that the triplets' mother had been featured in the year before, also thanks to Victoria.

Cobra took another sip of his drink. Neither he nor Colton had been surprised that Tez would be the first of the Masters triplets to walk down the aisle. The oldest triplet had never been a player, not in the true sense of the word. Although he had dated from time to time, his main goal in life had been to become a successful attorney.

When Cobra and Colton left Harvard after earning their bachelor's degrees to pursue graduate degrees elsewhere, Cortez had decided to remain at Harvard for law school. Then he had passed the bar on the first try.

Knowing how much time Tez had spent studying for that exam, Cobra and Colton had decided a "brothers' trip" to Paris was in order, where the three of them would celebrate. Tez had arrived in Paris a few days before he and Colton had, and that was when he had met Victoria Bennett.

Deciding to change the subject, Cobra said, "You gave a great Best Man speech, Tez."

"So did you."

Cobra shrugged. "Yeah, but I didn't say everything that I wanted to."

Cortez chuckled. "Colton and I are glad that you didn't. You've become unpredictable."

Cobra raised a questioning brow. "Unpredictable?"

Cortez nodded, smiling. "For the first time in your thirty-five years on this earth. It's starting to look like celibacy is getting to you."

He wouldn't admit it, even if it was. At least not to his brothers. "I will win the bet, Tez."

"Sure, you will," he laughed. "Just so you know, I've already decided where I'm going to take Victoria when I win those airline tickets off you."

"Don't waste your time. You won't be winning anything. Nor will Colt."

"Is that what you think, Cobra?"

"That's what I know, Tez."

"We'll see," his brother said, laughing again before he walked off.

***

Cobra watched his brother leave. Tez and Colt thought they knew him so well. So, okay, he'd admit the past seven months had been the hardest he'd ever had to deal with, and the next five would be torturous as fuck, but he would manage. Whenever he felt the need to bang his head up against the wall, while wishing he could bang into some woman's body instead, all he had to do was remember that night with Bernice. It made him angry every time he thought about it. What could she have gotten away with if he hadn't seen that video? That one night would have ruined him forever, had things gone her way.

Luckily, they hadn't.

And thanks to Cortez, the woman was now serving time. Since she had pleaded guilty, all that remained was the judge's sentencing. Cobra doubted he would ever forget that day. Her defense attorney, who had shown up in court a lot better dressed than he'd been that night, had pleaded for leniency, claiming this was Bernice's first mistake and that she was an excellent employee, a dedicated member of her church, and a good mother to her two little boys—ages two and three. Boys who would be placed in foster homes if Bernice went to prison. The woman had played her part by sobbing through most of the proceedings.

Cobra was glad that the stunt didn't work. Cortez had arranged for the fathers of Bernice's sons to appear at the hearing. Both wealthy men—one who played for the NFL and the other for the NBA—had stated that although they had no proof, they felt their one night with Bernice had been a similar setup.

Security cameras taken from the nightclubs where they'd met Bernice had shown she'd been wearing that same bracelet and decorative hairpin. That meant there was a good chance she had used both items before. After their one night with her, they hadn't heard from her again…until her lawyer had called to demand paternity tests.

The two men further stated that they would be glad to take full custody of their sons. Regardless of the circumstances surrounding their conception, both men stated that they loved their kids and could provide them with a better home. They would also make sure the brothers, who were only eleven months apart, got to spend time together.

Bernice Whey was given five years for sexual assault, with the intent to use a date-rape drug. And with the assault and battery charge brought about by Cobra, another year was added. Then, before the hearing ended, Cortez had brought down the final hammer—a move that Cobra hadn't known was coming.

It seemed Bernice had a third alias. Before moving to Savannah last year, she had lived in Seattle under the name of Lillie Dunkins. A warrant was currently out for her arrest for her involvement in an extortion ring that targeted wealthy men. She would invite them to her hotel room, where they were drugged and then videotaped having sex with her. The men would pay whatever she demanded to keep the video from being exploited.

The judge wasn't impressed. In addition to the sentence he had set, he stated that Allison, Bernice, Lillie, or whatever her real name was, would be extradited back to Seattle to face additional charges for her alleged crimes there. Since extortion was a federal offense, the FBI would handle the case.

While Cobra hadn't guessed the scope of Bernice's crimes, he wasn't surprised. Bernice had been quick to plead guilty—and she had done so for a reason. Cortez had suspected as much and asked Landon to do some digging. And he'd struck gold.

Angry at the way things had turned out for her, Bernice had gone berserk and began cursing out Cobra, Cortez, her two babies' daddies, and the judge. Before the bailiff could stop her, she slapped her attorney.

Her disorderly conduct and the assault on her attorney had resulted in her getting two more years added to her sentence. That meant she would have to serve time for a total of eight years, just for her crimes in Savannah. And there was no telling how many additional years she would receive for her part in the extortion ring in Seattle. Cobra didn't feel any pity for her. Not one iota.

After grabbing another drink off the tray of a passing waiter, Cobra glanced around the room. Once the newlyweds departed, he would decline any after-parties and go up to his hotel room to watch the NBA Finals on television.

He was about to take a sip of his drink when his gaze shifted, and he noticed a drop-dead gorgeous woman across the ballroom talking to Monica Bennett Chestnut. Who was she? She was the most gorgeous woman he had ever seen. That lime green gown complemented her golden-brown skin tone, and his fingers itched to touch the mass of brown hair that fell past her shoulders. She was too far away to determine the color of her eyes, but from where he stood, he could tell that her facial features were exquisite. And her gown was the perfect showcase for those vivacious curves. Yes, he definitely liked what he saw.

Because she had attended the wedding and seemed to know Monica, he could only assume she was a friend of Kelly's. Of course, Monica would know her as well, since she was Kelly's half-sister. Same father, different mothers.

Cobra checked his watch. He figured it would be another thirty minutes or so before the bride and groom reappeared. In the meantime, there was nothing wrong with moseying on over to where Monica and the woman were standing to get an introduction. Then again, maybe he shouldn't. He cursed his vow of celibacy. Spending too long in her presence would likely result in the worst kind of self-torture.

Out of the corner of his eye, he caught sight of Cortez, along with one of his best friends from Harvard Law School, Grant Corbain. They appeared to be heading toward where Monica and the woman stood. Cobra frowned. He liked Grant well enough, but he had seen the woman first. He didn't like the idea of Grant making a move just because Cobra was out of action...at least, for now.

Suddenly, he knew what he was going to do. He'd go over and say hello, then get the woman's contact information so he could call her later—like in five months.

That decision made, he strode across the room toward Monica's friend, making sure he'd be the man introduced to her first.

***

Desiree Sharpe was laughing at something Monica had shared with her when she noticed the man walking toward them. Although they hadn't met, she knew who he was—Cobra Masters. Brother of the groom—and the man she thoroughly detested, sight unseen.

He had somehow managed to develop a close relationship with her grandfather, something she'd never been able to do. Richard Sharpe had always been a detached man, reserved, and emotionally distant. At least, that was the way he'd always been with her. His own granddaughter.

She'd come from France to live with him when she was twelve, right after her parents had been killed in a boating accident. But instead of giving her the emotional support and love she had so desperately needed, he had immediately shipped her off to a boarding school in California.

She wasn't sure how he had managed it, but somehow Cobra Masters had breached Richard's tough, unemotional barriers, and he had become someone her grandfather enjoyed spending time with. She'd heard that they often played golf together and loved spending time on the water. She'd even heard that her grandfather had taught Cobra how to play chess, something he had refused to do for her, though she'd asked him more than once.

She broke eye contact with Cobra to glance down at the drink in her hand. Her grandfather had pointed him out to her earlier when he had been standing beside his brothers at the altar. He was an exceptionally good-looking man—tall, with beautiful brown skin, black hair that was cut short, dark eyes, dimples that appeared whenever he smiled, a neatly trimmed mustache, a bearded chin, and a nice physique. It had taken all of her concentration to keep her eyes off of him and pay attention to the wedding ceremony. With so many people there, she had hoped that their paths would not cross—at least not today. She could have used a little more time to prepare.

Still, she knew a meeting between them was inevitable. She'd returned home from France for good, so she'd be in the same town. And considering he was such a good friend of her grandfather, it was just a matter of time.

"Good evening, ladies."

Desiree glanced up and met his gaze. Great. There went any hope she had of avoiding him.

Up close, he was even more handsome. He smelled good as well. She was one of those women who loved the sensual and animalic scent of a man.

"Cobra," Monica said, giving him a hug. "Have you met Desiree?"

"No, I haven't," he said, extending his hand to her.

Desiree took it and felt his warmth. Immediately, a sizzling sensation passed through her body, but she was determined to ignore it. She had been around enough men to know when one was interested in her. However, most of the time, she hadn't been interested in any of them. Why was Cobra's very presence demanding that she make him an exception? One she had no intention of making. After all, she was determined not to like him.

"So, how do you know the bride and groom, Desiree?"

His pronunciation of her name had been perfect, especially when spoken in such a deep, sexy voice. She was about to answer when her grandfather and Monica's husband, Landon Chestnut, returned.

"Cobra, I see you've met my granddaughter."

Desiree watched Cobra's features go from surprise to utter shock. "Your granddaughter?" he asked, as his gaze moved from her grandfather to her and then back again. "I thought your granddaughter's name was Allison."

"I'm Allison Desiree Sharpe," she said, deciding to speak up for herself. "I was named Allison after my paternal grandmother, and Desiree after my mother. My grandfather calls me Allison, but I prefer to be called Desiree."

Cobra nodded. "I see."

She figured he understood perfectly. Her grandfather had never approved of her parents' marriage and, to this day, blamed her mother for her father's death. Years ago, she had been told by her mother's sister, Aunt Margot, that after a night of partying, her mother, who'd had too much to drink, had fallen off her parents' yacht somewhere in the waters of the French Riviera. Her father, who'd loved her mother very much, although he'd been just as drunk as his wife, jumped into the water to save her. Both had drowned.

"You should remember Allison," her grandfather said gruffly to Landon. "I hired your PI company to track her down that time."

"I do recall that assignment," Landon said. "It took me to St. Paul, and that's where I met the woman I would one day marry." Landon leaned over to place a kiss on Monica's lips, then added, "So, in the end, I'm very glad I took the assignment."

"Landon was hired to track you down?" Cobra asked.

Desiree shrugged, then said, "If he did, this is the first I heard of it."

"Why did you have her tracked down?" Cobra asked her grandfather, as if he had every right to know.

"Because I was notified by the college that she was missing. Of course, the first thing I assumed was that she had been kidnapped, so I called in the FBI. After their investigation, they determined there was no foul play. She had left of her own free will. That's when I hired Landon's PI firm to make sure, regardless of what the FBI said," her grandfather explained.

Cobra nodded again, then turned and met her gaze. "I take it you hadn't been kidnapped."

Desiree started to speak, but her grandfather beat her to it. "No, Allison hadn't been kidnapped. She'd wanted a break from school, and without letting me know of her plans, she left college in Memphis with two other girls. They took off for an entire semester, traveling all over the country just partying and having a good time."

She was more grateful than she cared to admit when Cobra changed the subject. "What school did you attend in Memphis?"

"Rhodes College."

"It's a liberal arts school, right?"

"Yes."

Of course, her grandfather was intent on putting his two cents in again. "I wanted her to go to Harvard," he said, disappointment evident in his voice. "Her grandmother and I graduated from there. So did her father."

Desiree scowled at her grandfather. "Too bad we can't always have what we want."

Like a young girl desperate for her grandfather's love, one who long ago accepted that she'd never have it, because her mother's blood also ran through her veins, Desiree thought.

"Allison, will you dance with me?" Cobra asked. When she narrowed her eyes, he amended his request, *"Desiree,* will you dance with me?"

She was tempted to refuse, telling him that she didn't want to do anything with him, but at that moment, she desperately needed to calm her nerves. Thanks to her grandfather, they were shot to hell.

He was so quick to point out anything she did wrong. Would he ever be proud of her for doing something right? While at Rhodes, she had made the Dean's List every single semester. Even after taking a semester off school, she'd still graduated on time with honors.

She nodded. "I'd like that."

Cobra smiled at her grandfather, Landon, and Monica, and said, "Please excuse us."

Then, taking Desiree's hand, he led her onto the dance floor just as the live band started playing a slow song.

24

CHAPTER 3

If Desiree's frown was anything to go by, Cobra could tell that she really hadn't wanted to dance with him, but had wanted to remain in her grandfather's presence even less. It was obvious the two didn't have much of a relationship. From the conversations Richard had shared with him, his granddaughter had been a handful while she was growing up. Cobra had gathered that instead of being firm, Richard had taken the path of least resistance and had catered to her every whim.

Now, after hearing how she'd taken a semester off school without bothering to tell her grandfather, causing him unnecessary stress and worry, he figured he'd been right. She was inconsiderate and selfish. Just the way he'd assumed her to be.

And what was there about the name Allison that seemed to bring out the worst in some women? First, there was Allison/ Bernice—the woman who was the cause of his current predicament. And now he'd met this Allison, who preferred to be called Desiree. Not that he had a problem with that—the name Allison left a bad taste in his mouth anyway.

Besides, the name Desiree suited her. Because something about her had desire sizzling through his veins. Talk about living up to a name; the first six letters of hers literally spell 'desire'.

As they moved to the music, she turned and met his gaze. She had the most beautiful hazel eyes he'd ever seen—a perfect blend of brown, green, and gold.

"Thanks for asking me to dance, Cobra."

He wished that he didn't like the way his name sounded on her lips. Her French accent was a turn-on. It wasn't too heavy, probably because she had moved to the States when she'd only been twelve. "Thanks for accepting. I should admit, though, that I did it more for Richard than for you. You should try not to aggravate him so much."

He could tell from her glare that she hadn't liked what he'd said. Unfortunately, a glare from those gorgeous hazel eyes just revved his libido, rather than put his bluntness in check. "And what about him aggravating me?" she asked in a clipped voice.

"He gets a pass."

Her glare deepened. "Why? Is it because he's one of your most important clients and you don't want to get on his bad side?"

If that was what she thought, she was definitely wrong. The reason he and Richard Sharpe got along so well was because Cobra wasn't anybody's 'yes' man—he wouldn't hesitate to tell Richard what he thought. The old man often told Cobra that he was the only snake he could trust. Cobra knew Richard wasn't used to being defied. But over the years, Desiree had obviously learned how.

"No. because at his age, he deserves peace rather than aggravation."

"Then maybe I should have stayed in Paris."

"Why didn't you?"

Cobra regretted asking the question the moment it came out of his mouth.

"It was time for me to come home."

He was surprised she answered his question, instead of telling him where to go.

"For your information, Cobra, my grandfather is the one who asked that I return. In fact, he practically demanded it. I can only assume he felt it was time I begin learning everything I can about the family business." She looked him up and down. "I start working at the Sharpe Corporation on Monday."

That was news to him. Although Richard had mentioned his granddaughter was coming home, Cobra had figured it would only be for a short visit and that she would be returning to Paris. Did that mean he would likely see her when he joined Richard for their Thursday night chess games? Or when Richard invited him to dinner? Damn, if that was the case, these next few months of celibacy might just kill him.

When they'd first met, Richard Sharpe had been a lonely man who reminded Cobra of his own grandfather, Kenneth Masters.

After divorcing wife number five, Kenneth had moved back into the community where wife number four—Cobra's grandmother —lived. He'd purchased a home on the same street. Of his five wives, she had been the only one to give him children...or so Kenneth had thought.

They had discovered just last year that his first wife had also borne him a child—a son that Kenneth had died not knowing about. The one thing Cobra would forever appreciate was the way their grandfather had taken an active role in their lives, even while married to wife number five. He figured he and his family were likely part of the reason the marriage hadn't lasted. The woman probably felt she couldn't compete against an ex-wife, four sons, and a slew of grandchildren. Not every woman could tolerate a man spending so much time with the family she had assumed he had given up.

But then, that was the thing—he never let go. He had always remained a part of their lives, and Cobra could honestly say Kenneth had been the grandfather his generation of Masters had needed. When he'd grown older, Kenneth had once admitted to Cobra that one reason he'd spent so much time with them was that he feared growing old alone.

And they had made sure he hadn't.

Cobra figured that he needed to keep Desiree talking so he wouldn't be tempted to notice how good she felt in his arms and how her scent was getting to him. He was familiar with several feminine fragrances but couldn't put a name to hers.

And focusing on her physical attributes was even worse. Her upper arms and shoulders, bared by the design of her gown, seemed to invite his touch. She appeared rather fit, and he wondered if, while living in Paris, she frequented the gym. And the low dip of her cleavage, exposing the top of her round breasts, made his mouth water.

"Anything else you want to know?"

His gaze reluctantly moved from her chest to her eyes, then shifted to her mouth, studying the sexy shape of it, wondering how good she would taste if he were to kiss her. So yes, there was more he wanted to know but dared not ask. At this point, his libido couldn't take any more.

"What are you going to be doing at the corporation?" he decided to ask, thinking it was a safe enough topic.

"What's wrong? You think I'll do something that will make the Sharpe stock go down? I understand your concern. After all, you are my grandfather's wealth and asset manager."

"I'm not worried at all. Richard has an excellent executive team, and they have many safeguards in place. It would take a lot more than something you do to make Sharpe Industries' stock collapse."

"It's good to know my financial future continues to be bright."

She sounded like someone who came from money. So far, his instincts were on target. "So how long do you plan to be in New York?"

"Any reason you want to know?"

"Just asking."

She nodded and then said, "For a while. I love New York. The one thing I regret is not getting to spend a lot of time here when I was young."

He frowned. "Didn't Richard get full custody of you when your parents were killed?"

"Yes, but I spent most of my time at a boarding school in California, and during the summers, I returned to Paris to visit my mother's sister, Aunt Margot."

He nodded. "But you did come home for holidays, right?"

"Yes, but do you know how many school holidays there are in a year, Cobra?"

Good question. He'd never had a reason to count. He and his brothers always looked forward to returning to Savannah whenever they got the chance. They still did. That was why, although they lived in various areas of the United States —Tez in LA, Colton in Boston, and he in New York —the triplets owned homes in Savannah, the most beautiful city in Georgia.

Knowing she was waiting for an answer, he said, "I never had a reason to count, actually."

"Well, I did."

Those words revealed a lot, whether she had wanted them to or not. Could there be more to this situation between Richard and his granddaughter? But then, he might be reading more into it. Hadn't she spent the last three years in Paris? According to Richard, she had taken off less than a week after graduating from college. Since she had no living relatives there —her mother's sister had died a few years ago in a car accident —Richard had assumed she had spent the past three years hanging out with friends.

"In a way, I'm glad that I'm back."

"Tired of partying in Paris, are you?"

He could tell his words had struck a nerve. Whatever blistering retort she was about to make was drowned out by the cheers and claps when Colton and Kelly reappeared dressed for travel, and looking like a couple madly in love and filled with extreme happiness. The music stopped, and everyone began moving toward them to see them off.

He turned to Desiree to suggest they follow the crowd, only to see her strolling off in the opposite direction without a backward glance.

***

Cobra seldom gave women a reason to walk away from him, and as far as he was concerned, he hadn't given Desiree one. Still, maybe it was a good idea to accept her actions as an omen. The last thing he needed was to spend time with a woman who'd make it impossible for him to think of anyone else. A woman who could test his ability to be in control... especially, of a locked zipper.

But then, maybe that was what he needed —a challenge. If he could resist the most beautiful creature he had ever seen, he'd know for sure that he'd win the bet with his brothers. And after all, there were still five months to go. And unless he cooled his friendship with Richard, temptation would undoubtedly eat him alive. Destroy the very essence of his being.

He didn't intend for that to happen, nor did he intend to cool his friendship with Richard. It was better to nip this in the bud. There was no way any woman, regardless of how beautiful, would get the best of him. After all, hadn't he and his brothers been called the Masters of the Game in high school for a reason?

Making a decision, he began walking in the direction Desiree had taken. Since most people were headed the opposite way, it wasn't long before he saw her. He quickly caught up with her. "Hey, where do you think you're running off to?" he asked, hooking his arm in hers.

When he turned her to him, he saw that she'd been crying. He frowned in concern. "Desiree? What's wrong?" Had what he'd said earlier offended her? The comment about her partying?

"Nothing is wrong," she said rather quickly. "Weddings make me weepy."

He thought there was more to it than that, but he'd take her at her word...or let her assume he did. "You're not alone," he said, steering her in the direction the other wedding guests were headed. "No doubt my mother, Inez Masters, is somewhere crying a river of happy tears right now. She's probably thinking, two sons down and one more to go."

He appreciated the sound of Desiree's chuckle. "She wants all her sons married?"

"Yes. That's her most ardent desire. Thank goodness she's never been desperate enough to play matchmaker. She believes true love will eventually find each of us, without her help. So far, it has for Tez and Colt."

"But not for you?"

"Mom knows it's just wishful thinking when it comes to me. Marriage isn't in my plans."

"It's not in mine, either."

Her words surprised him. "Really? I thought all girls dreamed of a day like this," he said, guiding her around several groups of people.

"I'm not one of them. And where are you taking me?"

"Closer to where the bride and groom are."

"Why?"

"I'm expected to be there."

"You, maybe, but not me," she said, pulling away slightly.

He loosened his hold on her arm, but didn't let go completely. "But at the moment you happen to be with me."

They walked over to where Kelly's mother and her husband stood. His parents, Cortez and Victoria, along with the rest of the Masters family, were close by. Cobra and Desiree arrived just in time to hear the last of his father's speech. His brothers looked at him, saw the way he'd hooked his arm in Desiree's, and smiled. Cobra frowned, knowing what they were thinking —that he wouldn't be able to resist temptation. He would let them think whatever they wanted. He knew better.

Desiree leaned in to ask, "Where are they going on their honeymoon?"

He moved closer to answer, realizing too late that it wasn't a good idea. The beauty of her hazel eyes was even more profound up close. "Maybe it would be better to ask where they aren't going. Colt has a four-week honeymoon planned, covering six countries—London. Ireland, Scotland, the Netherlands, Amsterdam, and Belgium.

"Sounds nice."

"I'm sure it will be. Here, I'll share my rice with you," he said, pulling a small pouch from the pocket of his tux.

"Thanks."

After tossing rice on the couple, Cobra and Desiree, along with the other wedding party and guests, watched as Colton and Kelly drove away from the wedding reception.

Once the car was no longer in sight, he turned to Desiree, wondering what to do. He knew what he *wanted* to do, but that was out of the question. Still, the wedding reception was over, and this was the time when they should part ways, but he wasn't quite ready.

He would forever be grateful to Richard for his timely appearance. "I've ordered the car to be brought around, Allison. The jet is fueled and ready to go," Richard said. Then he turned to Cobra, "You need a flight back to New York? If so, you can certainly join us."

"Thanks, Richard, but I'm fine," Cobra said, accepting that he had shared enough of Desiree's company today.

Richard nodded. "Then I'll see you Thursday for our chess game. Come early to dinner."

"I'll make sure that I do."

Cobra turned to look at the woman whose arm he was still holding. It was time to release it. "Thanks for the dance, Desiree."

"The pleasure was all mine, Cobra."

He chuckled—she was just being nice in front of Richard. But that was okay. In five months, Cobra was going to prove to her that the pleasure had been all his. And if he had anything to say about it, there would be a lot more of it. At least that was something he could look forward to.

***

Cobra heard a knock on his hotel room door. After glancing through the peephole, he opened it, then stood aside to let Cortez enter. "What do you want, Tez?"

"I thought I'd come keep you company for a spell."

Cobra rolled his eyes, crossing his arms over his chest as he leaned back against the door. "I'm going to tell you the same thing I told Straw, Tomb, and Titus. I don't want or need any company."

"You even said that to Savannah's mayor?" Cortez asked, grinning. "You must really have it bad."

"Whatever," Cobra said, leaving his place at the door to walk over to the love seat and sit down. "I know the only reason for your visit tonight is to see if you could catch a woman in my room."

Cortez chuckled as he eased down in the chair. "You are known to engage in that sort of thing after a wedding."

"That was before Bernice Whey. You made a trip here for nothing."

"It's never for nothing when I visit one of my brothers. Seriously, I just came to keep you company."

"And as I said, I don't want company."

Cortez chuckled. "Being horny has made you—"

"Unpredictable," Cobra interrupted. "At least that's what you said earlier."

"So, you admit to being horny?"

"No reason for me not to admit to it. I've never gone a month without getting laid, and going seven months is uncharted territory for me. But I'm managing." Then, to change the subject, Cobra asked, "So... Why are you here, keeping me company, and not with your wife?"

Cortez leaned back in his chair. "You know what it's like when the Bennett cousins get together. They'll watch a movie and catch up on all the family gossip."

Cobra nodded. Yes, he knew their routine. It always boggled his mind that three Masters men had married Bennett women. His cousin Quinn had married Alexia, his cousin Grey had married Brandy Bennett, and Cortez had married Victoria Bennett. Colton had come close. Although his wife, Kelly, was not a Bennett, she was a half-sister to Monica, who was a Bennett.

"So, who is the woman you were with earlier?" Cortez asked.

"Don't you know?" Cobra quipped.

Cortez shook his head. "I couldn't help but notice that you seemed to be holding on tight to her. And earlier, I saw the two of you dancing. So, to answer your smart-ass question, no, I don't know who she is."

"Her name is Desiree Sharpe."

Cortez sat up straight in his seat. "Sharpe? Is she Richard Sharpe's granddaughter?"

"Yes."

A frown appeared on Cortez's face, and he leaned back in the chair. "Shit. Then that's definitely a game changer."

Cobra raised a brow. "What are you talking about?"

"She's beautiful, and you're attracted to her. That much is obvious. I was hoping she would be the one who made you fall into temptation. But that won't be happening."

Tez was right. It wouldn't be happening. But he was curious as to why his brother was so sure of it. "And you're certain of that because…?"

Tez rolled his eyes. "You're an intelligent man, Cobra. Sometimes too intelligent for your own good. You're Sharpe's wealth and asset manager. Most of the man's portfolio is now being handled by Colt at Masters Unlimited. There's no way you would risk Richard Sharpe's ire by messing around with his granddaughter. His business is way too valuable for you or Colt to lose."

"I have no intentions of messing around with Desiree." *At least until his year of celibacy was over.*

"Thank goodness. I guess Colt and I will have to send more beautiful women your way to remind you of what you're missing."

"Don't waste your time. But I have to ask, why were you and Grant heading Desiree's way earlier, when she was talking to Monica? Was he vying for an introduction?"

"For your information, Grant and I were headed over to where Sherelle Telfair was talking to Brandy. Grant recalled meeting Sherelle at a party Lake gave in Orlando a couple of years ago, and I think he's interested in her."

Cobra nodded. Brandy Bennett Masters was married to their cousin Grey, and Sherelle Telfair had worked as a junior executive at Masters Unlimited, a marketing firm owned by their cousin Lake, with Colton as second-in-command. When Sherelle resigned last year, she was hired by the now Kelly Perkins Masters to manage one of Kelly's three consulting agencies.

"And where is Grant tonight?" Cobra asked.

"He caught a flight out after the reception for Memphis. He has a court case next week."

Because Cortez and Grant were best friends, most of the Masters knew the Corbains of Memphis. Grant's father was a judge, and his mother, Grant, and his three older siblings —Adam, Lincoln, and Sydney —were all successful attorneys in their family's law firm.

Cortez stood after checking his watch. "I'm to meet up with Quinn, Lake, and Grey for drinks at the bar. You're welcome to join us, if you want."

Cobra stood as well. "I'll pass. After the game, I'm going to bed—alone. I have an early flight home in the morning. But you and Victoria can expect a visit from me in a few weeks. It's been too long since I saw my nephew." He knew that Victoria's mom had flown to LA to keep her grandson while Tez and Victoria attended the wedding.

"Cornell is always glad to see his Uncle Cobra," Cortez said, giving his brother a bear hug. "Have a safe flight back to New York."

CHAPTER 4

Desiree walked into the office that would be hers and stopped in the doorway, a little stunned. She glanced around, certain that there had to be some mistake. Karlie Atworth, a Human Resources assistant, had taken her up to her own office, where Desiree had completed all the new-hire paperwork, and then the woman had given her a tour of the thirty-floor Sharpe Building. When they stopped at this office, Desiree didn't know what to say.

"Is something wrong, Miss Sharpe?"

She turned to Karlie, who looked like a high school student but had told Desiree she had graduated from NYU last year, and had been hired as an HR Assistant. Before answering, Desiree glanced around the office again and, this time, she noticed the nameplate on her desk. Allison D. Sharpe.

Legally, that was her name, so she shouldn't be too put out at seeing it. Besides, her best friend in the world, Camille LeGraff —a student by day and actress by night, would often ask her, in a Shakespearian accent, of course, *"Honestly, Rae, what's in a name?"*

And Desiree's answer would always be a quick, "Everything." She missed Camille already, although she'd only been back in the States for a week.

"Miss Sharpe?"

She then realized she hadn't answered Karlie's question. "No, nothing is wrong. I just wasn't expecting this."

Her office was just as spacious as her apartment in Paris. And the view of Manhattan was amazing. In her twenty-six years, she had only been to the Sharpe Building a couple of times, and she never recalled coming up to the fortieth floor.

"And why not?" Karlie asked her. "You are Richard Sharpe's granddaughter, right."

Richard Sharpe's granddaughter. She was certainly that, although she couldn't help thinking he forgot that at times. She nodded. "I am." There was no sense in telling Karlie that she was surprised because she'd told her grandfather that she'd be happy starting at the bottom and working her way up. So she'd been expecting a cubicle, not this spacious office.

Karlie nodded. "And speaking of Mr. Sharpe, you are scheduled to meet with him at two. His office is on this floor at the other end of the hall. If you need me to return and escort you there, I'll come back."

"No, that's okay. I'll find it."

"Alright. If there's anything you need, let me know. You will eventually be assigned your own administrative assistant, but in the meantime, I'm here to assist you."

Desiree glanced at her watch. "Since I have a three-hour wait before meeting with my grandfather, I would like to visit the company's library on the eleventh floor. Do I have access to it?"

"Yes, you have security clearance to all the floors in the building, except those privately leased."

Desiree nodded. "Thanks."

Once Karlie left, Desiree wandered around her office, not quite believing it was all hers. Out the window, she had a breathtaking view of Manhattan. She couldn't wait to start exploring...

Why did a vision of Cobra Masters suddenly pop into her mind? He was from New York, wasn't he? And as for breathtaking... She had to admit, she'd thought that same thing about him when her grandfather had pointed him out to her. In his tux, he had looked almost irresistible.

Releasing a frustrating sigh, she moved away from the window just as her cellphone started to ring. Recognizing the tone, she smiled. It was her best friend, Camille. Quickly pulling her phone out of her purse, she said, "Bonjour, Cam."

"Rae, how are things going?" Camille asked in her heavy French accent.

"Pretty well, so far. Are you just getting home from doing clinicals?" Camille had earned a degree in psychology and could open her own practice once her clinicals were completed.

"No. I'm getting ready to go to the theater. It's evening here. Have you forgotten about the six-hour time difference?"

Desiree slid down into the chair behind her desk. "Sorry, Cam," she said with a small groan. "I had."

"I figured as much. And before you ask, Rae, the answer is yes, I've memorized my lines, although I do miss you being here in Paris to coach me. How are you spending your day?"

"At the office. Granddad wanted me to start work today."

"How is that going?"

"I just got through new-hire orientation and have nothing else to do until I meet with him at two. Still, I'm a bit surprised."

"About what?"

"The size of my office. It's so spacious."

"Why wouldn't it be? You're your grandfather's only heir, Rae. And he obviously asked you to come home and learn about the family business for a reason."

"Yes, but…"

"But what?"

"I'm still not sure why he wanted me here. I don't think I'll be expected to do anything of vital importance. He has an executive team for that. One I understand is excellent," she said, remembering what Cobra had told her.

"And just think, you'll be running the place one of these days."

Since her grandfather had always said he had no intention of retiring, there was no way she'd be running the place until he was no longer here. And although they didn't have a great relationship, she didn't want to think of a time when he would not be around.

"When we first talked about it, I told him I wanted to learn the company from the ground up—maybe start off in the mail room. I figured I would have a cubicle or something. Definitely not the office I was given."

"Even if you are to learn the company from the ground up, Rae, that doesn't mean you will be doing the actual job. It merely means you will be exposed to it, seeing it, talking to people. And, of course, there'll be a job description manual."

"I haven't been given any manuals yet," Desiree said.

"I'm sure they're coming. So, what do you think of the Sharpe building?"

"It's very impressive. Different color schemes for every floor. A soothing atmosphere. The workspace is structured for functionality and productivity. An entire floor is a food court with various dining options if you prefer not to go out for lunch. And it even has a huge fitness center for the employees. A really nice one. I can't wait to check that out."

"Was your grandfather surprised when you told him what you've been doing for the past two-and-a-half years?"

"I didn't tell him. He thinks I was in Paris partying the entire time. To him, it's 'like mother, like daughter'."

"That's why I think you should tell him, so he'll know how wrong he is about you. But then, there's nothing wrong with enjoying your life every once in a while."

Although Desiree agreed, she knew her parents had taken 'enjoying themselves' to the extreme. Unfortunately, her grandfather still refused to accept that it hadn't only been her mother who'd liked to party. Her father had loved it just as much. Desiree could still remember how often—days, weeks, and sometimes months—they'd left her with Aunt Margot while they'd gone off somewhere with their friends.

"So, have you met Mr. Sharpe's financial planner?" Camille asked, intruding into her thoughts. "The one he spends a lot of time with?"

"The guy is his wealth asset manager."

"What's the difference?"

Desiree leaned back in her chair as she took off her earrings and placed them on her desk. "A financial manager only focuses on financial goal planning. On the other hand, a wealth asset manager deals with investments, tax strategies, and estate planning."

"Did you meet him?"

"Yes. I was Granddad's plus one at Cobra Master's brother's wedding this past weekend."

"And?"

"And what?" Desiree asked.

"Is he worth all that envious resentment you feel toward him?"

"Envious resentment?" Honestly, Cam, of all the people I could have chosen for a best friend, why did I pick a psych major?"

"I don't know. Why did you?"

"Not sure."

They burst out laughing, realizing the absurdity of their conversation. The moment Desiree had met Camille, they'd connected. It was as if they were sisters from different parents.

"Our couch misses you," Camille said, and Desiree could envision her best friend sitting there, trying to put on her makeup while wiping tears of laughter from her eyes.

"And I miss that couch. I don't want to think about how many times I'd lie there, letting you practice being my shrink."

"Practice makes perfect. And now, I have a degree on the wall that says I can open a private practice as a psychological therapist when I finish my clinicals."

"Do you think you'll do that, instead of spending so much time working nights as an actress?"

"Not sure, but then you know why, Rae."

"Yes, I do. Just like you know why I can't help but feel a little of resentment toward Cobra. We're hopeless."

"Hopeless but not helpless. I believe that one day we will have everything we want. Keep the faith."

"Easier said than done, kiddo. I'll let you go finish getting dressed. I don't want to be the reason you're late to the theater."

"Wait! I want to hear about that guy."

"He's the last person I want to talk about." Desiree paused. "Then again, I guess I could tell you some of the things I don't like about him."

"Like what?"

"He's very charming and confident."

"Nothing's wrong with that, Rae."

"I agree...if he's sincere."

"You don't think he is?"

"I honestly don't know. What I do know is that he is very good at persuading people to share his point of view."

"And you think that's what he's doing? Using his charm on your grandfather to persuade him to do whatever he wants?"

"Cobra is definitely a smooth operator. Not only does he have the gift of gab, but he's charismatic. *Too* charismatic."

"Hmmm... And is he good-looking?"

Camille's question made Desiree think back to her first impression of Cobra. He had been walking in her direction, and he'd had such a sexy and purposeful stride. There'd been so much masculinity in every step he took.

Like the other groomsmen, he had been handsomely outfitted in a black tux, but there had been something about him that made him stand out. It could have been his beard that gave him a rugged look, only adding to his sexiness. He hadn't been smiling nor had he been frowning. His expression was that of a man on the prowl, who'd seen something he wanted and intended to have it. If that was what he'd been thinking, he'd miscalculated when it came to her. If he didn't know how she felt about him when they parted ways last Saturday, she'd make sure to tell him if they ever ran into each other again.

"Rae?"

Startled, Desiree realized she hadn't answered her friend's question. "Yes, he is extremely handsome," she said truthfully.

"Were you attracted to him?"

Desiree decided there was no reason not to be completely honest. "Very much so."

"Then maybe it's not your grandfather you need to be concerned about. Maybe you're worried he'll manage to persuade you into doing something you won't want to."

"Don't worry about me, Cam. I can handle him."

"But why do you have to? He might be just what you need to prove Aimery wrong."

She wished Cam hadn't brought up the last guy she'd dated, a French racecar driver. Aimery had assumed that he was the hottest thing alive, both on and off the tracks. But in the bedroom, all his fire turned to smoke. The man was a lousy lover. And of course, when she hadn't climaxed during the one and only time they had made love, he had blamed it on her. Then, to add salt to the wound, as she was getting dressed to leave, he had picked up his cell phone and invited another woman to his bed.

"The last thing I need, at this moment in my life, is a man. Especially one like Cobra Masters."

"Then the only thing you have against him is his relationship with your grandfather?"

Desiree nibbled on her bottom lip. "To be honest, I don't have a problem with Cobra's relationship with my grandfather, as long as he doesn't have any ulterior motives. Is it wrong for me to want to make sure his actions are sincere?"

"Of course not."

Desiree was glad to hear that. She valued Cam's take on things.

"However," Cam added, "I wouldn't be so quick to judge. You should get to know him."

She wasn't so sure about that. "I don't know about that. Still, I'm glad I came home, so I can observe things for myself and intervene if I have to." She sighed. "I've told you enough about Cobra Masters. Call me tomorrow and let me know how the play goes tonight, okay? And Cam?"

"Yes?"

"I have a feeling that Léandre will soon realize how you feel about him. Find ways to let him know."

"Maybe he will, but right now, all Léandre cares about is his next production. In his mind, we're friends—good friends, but nothing more. Why do the men in our lives have to be complicated?"

"I'll let you figure that one out, since I don't have a man in my life, and I prefer to keep things that way."

After ending the call, Desiree stood, and when she did, she accidentally brushed the earrings she'd removed earlier off her desk, and they went tumbling to the floor. One fell under her chair, and the other rolled under her desk. "Dang." She got down on bended knees to retrieve them.

Getting the one from under her chair was easy. The challenge was recovering the one from under her desk. A few moments later, she succeeded. "Gotcha. It took me long enough to find you," she grumbled to herself, leaning back on her hunches to replace both earrings in her ears.

"And I wished it had taken you even longer," a deep male voice said behind her.

***

When Cobra had opened the door to Desiree's office, the last thing he expected to see was her on her knees, with her ass in the air. So, he had done what any other hot-blooded male would do—he'd silently ogled her. His gaze had taken in everything—the way her skirt hugged her figure, her graceful movements—and he'd immediately gotten hard.

He'd known she had a beautiful body. The sexy outfit she'd worn at Colton and Kelly's wedding had showcased it spectacularly. And now, seeing her on the floor, on her knees... It was doing crazy things to his already jacked-up libido. His favorite part of a woman's anatomy was her ass, and he could have stood there and stared at hers for hours.

To be on the safe side, he placed his briefcase in front of him, deliberately covering his crotch. And it wasn't a minute too soon, if the way Desiree glared at him over her shoulder was anything to go by. If looks could kill... A lesser man would have high-tailed it out of her office.

"You have a problem with knocking, Cobra?"

"I did knock. I guess you didn't hear me."

"That doesn't mean you can just come in."

"I thought you weren't here and was going to leave a note on your desk."

When she made a move to get off the floor, he walked over to her and presented his hand. "Here, let me help you up."

From the way she looked at his hand before taking it, he thought she'd decline his help, but then she placed hers in his. The moment she did, that same intense sensation he had felt when they shook hands at the wedding reception rushed through him. That had to be why he went still and stood there staring down at her, holding her hand instead of helping her up.

A frown settled on her lips. "Are you going to help me up or not?"

Her cutting words broke the passionate spell that had captivated him, and he helped her to her feet, but didn't let go of her hand until she pulled it away. "Thanks. So, why are you here, Cobra?"

He took a few moments to gather his wits before he answered. "I had a meeting with Richard earlier. I recalled you saying today would be your first day, so I asked him about you, and he told me where your office was located." Glancing around, he said. "Nice view!"

She followed his gaze. "That's what I thought when I first saw it." Going around her desk, she slid into the chair. He had watched her every move, thinking she had both the curves and the legs for that skirt. Pencil skirts had a way of showcasing a woman's best attributes, and Desiree was certainly a boss in hers. "You haven't said why you're here."

Although she hadn't asked him to sit, he slid into a chair and placed his briefcase across his lap. "As I said, I had a meeting with Richard. I remembered that you were starting work today, and thought I'd check in and see how things were going." There was no way he would admit that he had thought about her a lot since he last saw her.

She nodded. "So far so good. I have a meeting with Granddad in a couple of hours. Do you normally see him on Mondays?"

"Not always," Cobra replied. "We meet at least once a month or as needed. He uses his company's fitness room a lot in the morning, and oftentimes I join him. We occasionally meet up on the weekends to go boating, play golf, and play tennis."

"My grandfather plays tennis?"

"Sure does. Like a champ. Any reason he shouldn't? He's only sixty-three."

She narrowed her gaze. "Are we talking about the same man? Because just last Saturday, you told me that he deserves peace instead of aggravation because of his age."

"Yes, and I still stand behind what I said. Sixty-three is old but not ancient, Desiree. I try to encourage Richard to stay active and eat healthy in order to live longer. I'm sure you want him to stay around as much as I do."

"He's my grandfather, so of course I care about his health and well-being. But I'm wondering what's in it for you?"

Her question pissed him off. He didn't say anything for a minute, mainly because he wasn't exactly sure what to say. Finally, he looked her in the eye and said, "This is the second time you've implied—in a roundabout way—that my concern for Richard is not genuine, and I don't like it, nor do I appreciate it. I don't know what your problem is, Desiree, or why you're questioning the sincerity of my friendship with your grandfather. Are you feeling guilty because I was here for him while you spent almost three years having a good time in Paris?"

She leaned over her desk, her hazel eyes blazing with fire. Why did the thought of seeing that degree of fire in the bedroom suddenly flash through his mind? "You know nothing about me or what I was doing in Paris."

He got out of his seat and leaned in toward her. Their noses were close to touching. "And you know nothing about me. Whether you like it or not, my friendship with your grandfather is solid, and there's not a damn thing you can do about it."

Then, without saying another word, he walked out of her office.

CHAPTER 5

"I'm here to see Mr. Sharpe."

The older woman behind the desk looked up at Desiree through wide-rimmed glasses, studied her features intently, then smiled. "Allison, we finally meet."

From the sound of her voice, Desiree knew the person staring up at her was Eloise Markam, her grandfather's administrative assistant for the past fifteen years. Although they had never officially met, Eloise was the one who would take messages and pass them along to her grandfather whenever Richard Sharpe was too busy to talk.

Those were the days Desiree would call from boarding school, asking him to add more funds to her charge cards. Back then, she had to admit, she'd thought of her grandfather more as her banker than her guardian. She recalled one phone call in particular. Ms. Markam had obviously assumed she had placed Desiree on hold, but she hadn't. Desiree had overheard her tell whoever she'd been talking to that Mr. Sharpe's spoiled, bratty granddaughter only called when she wanted something. Then she'd followed up by saying some other not-so-nice things about her.

Then, while in college, Desiree had often called her grandfather, especially after her Aunt Margot had passed away. It was during those times she had felt most alone and needed to hear his voice. However, Eloise Markham was quick to say he was busy and would let him know she called, but he never called back.

"Yes, we finally meet." Still reeling from her angry exchange with Cobra, which had left her frustrated, and now remembering the horrible things Eloise had said that day, propelled Desiree to say, "You can tell Mr. Sharpe that his spoiled, bratty granddaughter has arrived for their two o'clock meeting."

An embarrassed look appeared on the woman's face.

Desiree suddenly felt bad. This was no way to make a first impression. So, to make light of what she'd said and to let Eloise know she'd gotten over that time as well as the description, Desiree chuckled and said, "I admit I was quite a handful then. But I can assure you those days are over."

"I'm sure they are," Eloise said softly, coming to her feet. "I will announce you to Mr. Sharpe."

"Thank you, Eloise." Desiree watched the woman quickly walk away.

Announce her? Richard Sharpe should have been expecting her, so why didn't Eloise just say, "Go right on in?"

Come to think about it, Desiree couldn't remember a single time when she had called her grandfather, and Eloise had put her through to him directly. The woman had taken a message every time, as if she was his guard dog or something. Was she still doing that?

"Mr. Sharpe will see you now."

Desiree smiled at Eloise. "Thank you. And by the way, I remember calling my grandfather one time when I was in college. I'd decided to sit out a semester and had asked him to call me. I found out this weekend that he never got that message."

Desiree could see the color nearly drain from the woman's features. "I don't remember that, Allison."

"Then it's a good thing that I do, Eloise."

She then walked off.

***

Upon entering her grandfather's office, Desiree glanced around. It was four times the size of hers, perfectly furnished and accessorized to represent the company's CEO. And the view outside his wall-to-wall window of the Manhattan skyline was even more breathtaking than the view in her office. She would consider spending the nights here just to wake up to that stunning sight. And standing in front of that window was Richard Sharpe.

Her grandfather had always seemed larger than life to her. Now, he was older—all that black hair was now sprinkled with gray—and she inwardly cringed at the thought that she might have been responsible for more than a few strands. But still, she would have to say, he had aged with grace and dignity. He still had a stately yet commanding presence about him. He stood tall, confident, well-groomed, and distinguished-looking. She could even go so far as to say her grandfather was a handsome man. His eyes, timelessly sharp and keen, signified a high intelligence.

He didn't have many wrinkles on his face for a man his age, and he appeared to be in good physical shape. But then, hadn't Cobra said he even played tennis? She hadn't considered that he'd be that active before, but could definitely see it now.

Her aunt had kept copies of the international magazines that had showcased his work, featuring him on the covers when he'd been younger. He had been described as a visionary, an industrial tycoon, someone cool under fire. No doubt he had wanted to pass on those same characteristics to his son, who he had expected to take over the company one day. Instead, his son lived a little too large and nearly bankrupted their Paris office. And now, she could tell that Richard believed she'd do the same thing. But she was determined to prove him wrong.

"Welcome to the Sharpe Corporation, Allison."

"Thanks for hiring me."

"Did you think that I wouldn't?" he asked, moving away from the window to stand by his desk.

"I guess not, after demanding I come home and take on my responsibility as a Sharpe."

If her words annoyed him, he didn't show it. "Please have a seat, Allison. And you look very nice today."

Had he thought she would wear jeans and a t-shirt? Or worse, something one would usually wear to a nightclub?

Early on, he had set the tone he preferred for the Sharpe Corporation and, over the years, hadn't changed it. It was strictly professional, with no aberrations. So, she had laid out her clothes last night—a black pencil skirt, white blouse, and a black, white, and gray plaid blazer with closed-toe pumps with what would be considered an appropriate heel. She wasn't going to give him a chance to disapprove of her on her first day.

"Thank you," she said, taking the chair in front of his desk.

"So, what do you think of the place so far?" he asked, sitting down as well.

"I took a tour earlier. It's a nice building. However, it's too early to comment on your business model or the company's environment until I become more familiar with them."

She could see the surprise on his face. No doubt he was wondering how she was familiar with such things...which told her that he had no idea about what she could do. It was too bad he hadn't bothered to keep up with her activities the last three years.

Not to give him such time to speculate, she said, "I told you I wanted to learn every aspect of the company from the ground up. So why do I have an office on the fortieth floor?"

He leaned back in his seat. "You're a Sharpe," he answered as if that was reason enough. "However, I will comply with your request and make sure that during your first month here, you will engage in extensive cross-training."

"Good. Anything else?"

"Eloise will be assigning an administrative assistant to you sometime today."

"I'd rather select my own."

He lifted a brow. "Any particular reason why?"

There was no need to tell him that she figured anyone Eloise would assign would only serve as a spy. "I just do. I like the young lady who assisted me earlier, Karlie Atworth."

"What do you know about her?" her grandfather asked, writing the name on a notepad.

"Other than she graduated from NYU last year and was hired here shortly after that, and is currently an HR Assistant, basically nothing. However, I feel she can be trusted. And trust is important to me."

He stared at her, and she stared back, not caring how he interpreted the statement. "I'll have Eloise contact the HR Director and let her know."

"Thank you."

'By the way, did Cobra find your office?"

"Yes, he found it."

"Good."

"Not sure if it was good or not, especially for him."

Richard Sharpe frowned. "What do you mean?"

She shrugged. "I might have offended his sensibilities."

Her grandfather chuckled. The sound surprised her. She couldn't recall a time she'd heard him laugh. Around her, he was always serious. "Offended his sensibilities? I know Cobra a lot better than you do, and he can hold his own, trust me."

"Well, I don't particularly like him."

He chuckled again. "Then I guess it's a good thing he's not trying to win a popularity contest."

Desiree pretended to pull a non-existent thread on her jacket. "You obviously like him." She knew that he did, but wanted to see if her opinion of Cobra had any bearing on him.

"Yes, I like him. I also respect him. And I often tell him that he's the only snake that I trust. A cobra is a venomous snake that raises its hood when threatened. It serves as a defense mechanism. They don't take intimidation well."

She wondered if her grandfather was telling her that for a reason. In case he was, she said, "And I'm a Sharpe. I possess an edge that can cut things into pieces. Even venomous snakes."

Desiree actually smiled at the thought of that, and some of the anger and frustration she'd felt since her disagreement with Cobra eased out of her.

Standing, she said, "Thanks for meeting with me. Unless there is something else, I'll return to my office now."

"Not right now, no."

Nodding, Desiree walked out.

***

"You weren't in the best mood this weekend, Cobra, so I thought I'd brighten your day by sharing some news that came across my desk this morning."

Cobra slid into the chair behind his desk. "There was nothing wrong with my mood this weekend, Straw."

"Uhm, yeah, there was. And I know why. Celibacy can take a huge toll on a guy."

Cobra didn't want to talk about it. "What news do you have?"

"Allison, aka Lillie, whose legal name is Bernice Whey, was sentenced to ten years for her involvement in that extortion ring. It seems the FBI case against her was bulletproof."

Cobra released a whistle. "That's a total of eighteen years. Sad but well-deserved."

"I'm just glad her sons are with their fathers, who will take good care of them," Straw said.

"Yeah. Maybe it all worked out for the best, at least for the kids. By the way, I meant to ask you how Paula was doing. I know you asked her to come as your plus-one, but she couldn't make it."

"Her mother was sick. Came down with a virus or something."

"How is Mrs. Costner doing now?"

"A lot better. That's the other reason I'm calling. I asked Paula to marry me last night, and she said yes."

Cobra grinned. "Congratulations. It's about time, don't you think?"

"Yeah, man. It's definitely time," Straw agreed. "I've been given a second chance, and I don't plan to mess this up.

Paula and Straw had dated in high school, but they'd gone their separate ways when they'd left for college. They eventually married other people and later divorced. Straw had moved back to Savannah ten years ago to become sheriff, and Paula returned two years ago, accepting the job of dean of the Business Department at Savannah State University.

Cobra had always liked Paula and thought Straw had made a mistake when he'd broken up with her at the end of their final year in high school. He'd always hoped the two would get back together, but then they'd ended up marrying others. However, when she returned to town, he'd had kept his fingers crossed.

"So, when is the wedding, Straw?"

"The last weekend in September. Will you be my best man?"

"Of course, I'll be by your side. As I said, it's about time."

"Yes, it is. I should never have broken up with her all those years ago. I'm just glad we found our way back to each other."

"I am too."

"Of course, Mom is overjoyed. She always liked Paula. From the beginning, she thought Jasmine only married me because she thought I was headed to the NBA. When she divorced me, she proved Mom right.

"All that is behind you now. I can see you having a great future with Paula."

"I can, too. We've even talked about having a family."

Cobra grinned, envisioning a lot of little Straws running around.

"So, the way I see it, Cobra, there's hope for you. It's never too late to find the girl of your dreams."

Cobra rolled his eyes. "Not looking for her. I like my life just the way it is. And I'm going to like it even more when I get beyond that damn year of celibacy. I need to get laid badly."

"Don't. Or you lose the bet."

"Don't worry. There's not a woman alive who will make me lose that bet. Not a single one..."

At that moment, the memory of seeing Desiree on her knees, looking for her earring, flashed in his mind. He cursed under his breath when he felt his penis get hard at the thought.

"Alright, I'll let you get back to work now, Cobra."

"Thanks, Straw. And again, congratulations to you and Paula. Give her my love, will you?"

"Absolutely."

Cobra leaned back in his chair after his call with Straw ended. He'd honestly not thought Desiree Sharpe could dominate his thoughts the way she was doing. Granted, he'd had a meeting scheduled this morning with Richard, but he hadn't needed to seek her out afterwards. He'd regretted that visit ever since. The nerve of her assuming he'd become friends with Richard just for what he could get out of it. That meant she honestly didn't know her grandfather well at all. Richard wasn't a man to be taken in by false flattery or persuasion. He was too intelligent to allow that to happen.

Of course, her words also told Cobra exactly what she thought about his character. Did he care? Not really. She didn't know him, and he certainly didn't know her. And after this morning, he didn't think he wanted to. If she could question his motives, why couldn't he question hers? Granddaughter or not.

Granted, she said she'd returned to the States because Richard had demanded it. Knowing Richard, Cobra had no doubt of it. However, if she was rebelling against being told what to do, how far would she go? Would she deliberately defy authority? Drive the grandfather who loved her into having a heart attack?

There was no doubt Richard loved his granddaughter. Although he'd been annoyed at some of the things she had done over the years, Cobra could still hear a grandparent's love in his voice whenever he spoke of her. He recognized it because he'd heard it in his own grandfather's voice.

Richard and Desiree definitely had issues they needed to resolve, but it was up to them to rectify them—not Cobra.

However, he wasn't about to sit by and watch her cause Richard undue stress. That meant Cobra needed to find out as much about Desiree, and her game plan, as he could. What had she been doing in Paris for the last three years? Who had she spent time with? Was there a man in her life? He quickly dismissed that thought. He didn't care.

Picking up his cell phone, he called Landon Chestnut.

Landon picked up on the first ring. "Cobra. What can I do for you?"

"I need you to tell me everything you can find out about Allison Desiree Sharpe."

"You want her investigated?"

"Yes."

The phone got quiet, and then Landon said, "I shouldn't ask, but why?"

"I don't trust her."

Landon chuckled. "You seemed pretty trusting of her while the two of you were dancing at Colton and Kelly's wedding reception. And afterwards, you were holding onto her so tightly, it looked as if you didn't want to let her go."

"I wasn't holding on that tight."

"Okay, if you say so, but you were noticed. Even Monica mentioned it."

"Your wife sees too much. Just do what I'm hiring you to do, will you?"

"That's fine with me. I just hope what you're doing doesn't come back to bite you in the ass." He paused, and Cobra could hear him flipping through some papers. "Okay, I'm working on a case that I should have wrapped up in a few weeks, and then I'll be free to help you out."

"That's great. Thanks."

And it was. Because he knew Landon would leave no stone unturned. In a few weeks, he'd know everything there was to know about Desiree Sharpe.

***

On her way back to her office, Desiree stopped by the ladies' room. She loved how elegant the restrooms on the executive floor were designed, especially the way the stalls were divided into private compartments. Each one was completely enclosed with a full-height door.

She had just entered one of the compartments when she heard two women whispering as they entered after her. Obviously thinking that they were alone, their voices raised to a normal pitch. She ignored their conversation until she heard one woman mention Cobra's name.

"Are you sure, Mary Anne?"

"Positive. It happened sometime last year, early November. My cousin, who lives in Savannah and works at the courthouse, gave me the scoop."

Scoop? Desiree decided to listen to what the women were saying, especially if Cobra was involved in some scandal.

The woman continued, "Cobra Masters took a woman he met in a bar home with him, and she tried to trap him by putting a drug in his drink and punching holes in the condoms he'd intended to use. He caught her doing it, had her arrested, and now she's serving time."

"It's a good thing he caught her. Can you imagine what would have happened if he hadn't?" the other woman replied.

"His life would have been ruined. I understand he was so upset by it that he's vowed to go a full year without sex."

"Cobra Masters? The king of one-night stands, isn't sleeping around? You've got to be kidding. I have trouble believing that's actually possible. There are going to be a lot of unhappy women around here, if that's the case. I've heard he's incredible in the bedroom. Are you sure?"

"According to my cousin, whose brother is a good friend of Cortez's, the three brothers even made a bet that he could last a year without sex. And supposedly, he's winning the bet so far, and only has a few more months to go."

"Personally, I don't think he'll last," one woman said, chuckling.

"Me neither," the other one replied.

The two women finally left the ladies' room without using it. It was only then that Desiree came out. As she stood at the sink to wash her hands, she thought about what she had overheard. It was a good thing the woman who had tried to trick Cobra had gotten caught. What kind of woman thought of something like that?

She was also interested that neither woman thought he would last a year of celibacy. From the sounds of it, he had a reputation for being the king of one-night stands. Well, what he did or what he didn't do was no concern of hers.

However, his relationship with her grandfather was. And if getting to know him better was the only way to put her doubts to rest about his motives, she'd would try to get along with him, even if it killed her. And it might.

CHAPTER 6

Cobra studied the chessboard. Richard had been trying all night to trap him, but he wasn't having it. He refused to be baited, even by the man who had taught him everything he knew about the game.

"I understand my granddaughter doesn't like you much," Richard said.

Cobra didn't bother to look up because he knew Richard hadn't. One of the rules the older man had instilled in him was that, unless you needed to rest your eyes for a minute, a good chess player knew not to take their eyes off the board for long.

"To be honest, Richard, I don't care much for your granddaughter either. She accused me of trying to use you."

"She said that?" Richard asked, as if surprised.

"Twice. Once at the wedding and then at her office on Monday. That pissed me off."

Richard chuckled. "I'm sure it did."

"Where is she, by the way?" Cobra asked, glancing around. When he decided to join Richard for dinner before their chess game, he'd assumed she would be there. The fact that he didn't like her meant nothing. If anything, he'd hoped his presence would annoy her.

"Allison is still at the office. She wants to get through all those manuals she has to read."

Cobra nodded. "How late will she be working?"

"If she follows the same pattern as the other couple of nights, I would say until around ten."

"Ten? And how will she get home?"

"I usually send my car for her. However, I don't think she appreciates it. I guess it rains on her independence. Although this place is plenty big enough, I have a feeling the only reason she's staying here and not moving into an apartment is that she thinks she needs to keep an eye on me." Richard smiled as if he found the very thought amusing.

Cobra rolled his eyes. "Or so she can keep an eye on your friends and associates, so they don't take advantage of you. As if such a thing were possible. I'm convinced the older you get, the sharper you get."

"I'm glad you think so. Checkmate."

Cobra blinked. How had he let that move happen? Damn, he had become trapped after all. "As I said, the older you get, the sharper you get," he said, standing and putting on his jacket. "When will Lolita be returning?"

"Not for another month. She is enjoying spending time with her daughter, son-in-law, and grandson in Sydney over the summer. I'm thinking of joining her there for a couple of weeks."

Lolita Albritton was the woman Richard had started dating a year ago. The two had met when Lolita and Richard had attended a special party in honor of New York's new mayor. Lolita was a widow who had taken over the running of her husband's media business upon his death. She'd retired two years ago and had turned over the running of the corporation to her son.

In Cobra's mind, Richard and Lolita were compatible on so many levels. They shared a number of values and interests. Richard had confided that he never thought he would meet a woman who could hold a light to his wife, but he had. He wondered if the real reason Richard had requested that Desiree return to the States was to meet Lolita. "Have you told Desiree about her?"

"Not yet, but I plan to do so soon."

Cobra nodded. "Thanks for dinner."

"Anytime."

Before reaching the door, Cobra turned and said, "How about calling Ron to cancel that pickup."

Richard lifted a brow. "Why?"

"I'll pick Desiree up and bring her home. Can you call your night security station to approve my access to the fortieth floor?"

Richard eyed him curiously. "I thought you and Allison didn't like each other."

"We don't. However, after losing to you tonight, I'm in the mood to annoy somebody." He crossed the room, opening the door to leave. "Goodnight, Richard."

***

Desiree heard the knock on her office door and looked up from the manual she'd been studying. The cleanup crew had already made their rounds, so she wondered who it could be. According to Karlie, very few people worked late on this floor. Obviously, someone had.

"Come in."

The door opened, and Cobra Masters walked in. She tightened her mouth, mainly from keeping her jaw from dropping.

What on earth was he doing here? And at this hour? How had he gained access to this floor?

Her grandfather had mentioned that he and Cobra were playing chess tonight. So, what was he doing here, in her office, leaning against the door and studying her with those intense dark eyes? It was obvious he was waiting for some sort of reaction from her. Considering how their last encounter ended, was he expecting her to throw something at him?

Desiree doubted it. In fact, he was standing there looking just as cool and calm as anyone could in a shirt, jeans, and a lightweight jacket that accentuated his broad shoulders and firm abs. Why did he always look so sexy? It didn't seem to matter if he was wearing a tux, a business suit, or a pair of jeans. He was too attractive, and it bothered her that she was too aware of him.

"What are you doing here, Cobra?"

He walked away from the door to sit in the chair across from her desk. She watched him, tuned into his every move. What was it about him that moved her? Her heart was racing, and her breathing seemed to catch, all because he was here. She resented her body's reaction to him and desperately hoped he wouldn't notice.

"I don't recall inviting you to sit down," she said.

"You didn't. And to answer your question, I played chess with Richard tonight, and he told me you were working late."

"And that concerned you how, exactly?" Desiree asked.

"Honestly, it doesn't."

"Then why are you here?"

***

Cobra could give her a lot of reasons, but most would amount to nothing but bullshit. Even the reason he had given Richard was crap. For some reason, which he clearly hadn't figured out, he was attracted to her, and it couldn't have happened at a worse time. Had he met her last year, that would have been great. He could even envision her being someone he took to bed more than once. And that said a lot for someone who was a one-and-done man.

However, there was no way he would tell her the truth about why he was here. That she had been on his mind more often than he liked. That he'd woken up in the middle of the night twice this week with a hard-on from hell as a result of dreaming about making love to her. And he'd never lost a good night's sleep over a woman.

He blamed it on the bet he'd made with his brothers. Or, more fitting, he blamed it on Bernice Whey, and her many aliases.

"I'm waiting, Cobra."

He shifted in his seat, hoping she wouldn't notice how aroused he'd become just from looking at her. That was the reason he'd needed to sit down. The moment he'd walked in and saw her sitting there, a rush of want and need had raced through him. What woman would still look so good this late at night? One who was so well put together? Whose beauty was so striking? Who didn't have a strand of hair out of place? Damn, even that red lipstick on her lips looked fresh.

"I thought I'd take you home."

She lifted a brow. "Any reason Ron isn't coming?"

"I told Richard to cancel Ron, that I would do it."

She narrowed her gaze. "Did it at any time occur to you that I'd prefer not to see you?"

He smiled. "Of course. But I wasn't going to let that stop me."

There was no reason to tell her that he had called himself all kinds of a fool on the elevator ride up to this floor. But the moment he had walked in and seen her, he had realized that coming here made perfect sense. Especially to a man who was one of the masters of the game. With his brothers married, he was the last one—a man who viewed romantic pursuit as a strategic "game" to be won.

Bottom line, he wanted her in his bed. However, it would be another five months—inching toward four—before he could make such a thing happen. In the meantime, he saw no reason not to use this time to prime her for what was to come. That way, when it happened, she would want him as much as he wanted her. He would see to it.

"So why are you here?"

"Do you want a truthful answer?"

"I don't just want a truthful answer, Cobra, I expect one."

He nodded. A master of the game could answer a question truthfully, but in a way so as not to reveal their strategy. "The reason I'm here has everything to do with your mouth, Desiree."

She chuckled at that. "What's wrong with my mouth? Is it too sassy for you? Are you one of those men who dislike outspoken women? A woman who can hold her own?"

"It's none of those things."

He was tempted to smile at the confused look that appeared in her features. "Then what are you talking about?"

He studied it for a moment. "I think you possess the most tempting pair of lips I've ever seen on a woman." And he had a feeling that one day, that mouth would be his downfall.

She stared hard at him for a second, and then burst into laughter. He loved the sound of her laughter, but wondered what the hell she found so amusing?

"Is that the best pickup line you've got? Honestly?"

He shrugged. "It wasn't a pickup line."

"Then what was it?"

"The truth. Your lips are full and plump. The shape of your mouth is perfect for your face."

She rolled her eyes. "Do you honestly want me to think you cancelled my ride with Ron because of your fascination with my mouth?"

"It's more than a fascination, Desiree, trust me."

He could tell from the look in the depths of her hazel eyes that he definitely had her attention now. "Then, what is it?"

That answer was easy. "A desire that I can't seem to kick."

"A desire to do what?"

"To kiss you."

***

Desiree felt her breath catch in her lungs, and she had to force herself to breathe. She frowned at Cobra, wondering what game he was playing. Hadn't he taken a vow of celibacy? If that was true, he sure wasn't acting like it. But then he hadn't asked her to share a bed with him. He only wanted a kiss.

"Have you forgotten we don't like each other?" she asked. He thought her mouth was fascinating. She could certainly say the same about his.

"I think we can put the dislike aside for one kiss, Desiree."

"What makes you think I want to kiss a man I don't even like?"

A smile touched the corners of his lips. "You might not like me, but you'll like my kiss."

This was madness. She should ask him to leave, then call her grandfather and ask for Ron to pick her up as planned.

What was Cobra thinking, showing up here with such foolishness on his mind? All that confidence and charm had gone to his head. Did he think she would be so easily persuaded to give him whatever he wanted?

"And what if I don't like it?"

"You will."

God, Cobra was as conceited as they came. In fact, his arrogance reminded her of Aimery's. But then, according to what the women in the ladies' room said, it seemed that, unlike Aimery, Cobra was a good lover. An incredible one, even.

"You are so sure of yourself, aren't you?"

"Let's just say I've never heard a woman complain."

Desiree thought back to how it had been with Aimery. She'd actually thought herself frigid for a while. Thanks to Camille, she had discovered that several women had a lot to say about Aimery's selfishness in bed, but he never knew because they faked their orgasms. The last thing they wanted was to miss out on all the lavish gifts he often gave his lovers. She hadn't needed or wanted his gifts and had refused to fake anything in the bedroom.

"A lot of men think they're hot simply because very few women have the courage to tell them they are not," she said.

By his frown, she could tell he didn't like her questioning his virility. "Do you want me to prove it?" he asked.

Desiree rolled her eyes. "Seriously? You just met me Saturday, Cobra, and today is Thursday. We haven't even known each other a week."

"And that's supposed to mean something? I'm not asking you to go to bed with me, Desiree. All I want is a kiss."

Although he didn't know it, she knew why he wasn't trying to sleep with her. The conversation she'd overheard that day in the ladies' room had been fortuitous. Still, she couldn't resist asking, "And what if you can't stop after a kiss, Cobra?"

"I'll stop, trust me."

"You sound pretty sure of yourself."

"No reason for me not to be."

She held his gaze for a moment. "So you don't think I'm capable of driving you insane with desire? Of pushing you over the edge of lust to the point of no return?" Although Aimery had claimed she'd lacked skills in the bedroom, he'd always seemed to enjoy her kisses.

Cobra stood and slowly walked over to her desk, standing beside her chair. Her heart rate had increased with every step he took. "There is no doubt in my mind that I'll likely want more than a kiss, and there's a strong chance I'll be tempted to talk you into giving me more. But I won't."

"Why not?" she asked. Would he tell her the reason?

"Because all I want to do is kiss you."

"Is the fact that I'm Richard's granddaughter stopping you from wanting more?"

"No. You're an adult who can make your own decisions. I believe Richard would respect that."

Desiree believed that as well. But he still wasn't giving her a straight answer—the answer she already knew. To him, this was all about emotional gaslighting—a type of psychological manipulation that some men used. Thanks to Camille, Desiree knew more about the workings of the human mind than most people.

Right now, she wasn't sure just what he was up to or what nonsense he was thinking of using on her. But whatever his plan, Cobra would soon find out she was a worthy opponent. She was a Sharpe. And it wasn't just her name. Like the other definition of 'sharp', she was quick-witted, perceptive, and able to think on her feet. And she wasn't afraid to draw blood.

Pushing her chair back, she stood in front of him. When he took a step toward her, she held her ground. "One kiss, Cobra, and that's it."

A smile touched his lips. "One kiss, Desiree, unless you ask for more. However, I give you my word, kisses are all we will share. I won't take you on this desk. No matter how tempted I might be."

"Take me on this desk? Hmmm... Why not? It sounds rather intriguing."

He stared at her, and she could tell her response hadn't been what he'd expected. He'd obviously assumed she would resist such an idea, at least display indignation that he had said such a thing, but she hadn't. Her accepting attitude to what he'd said had surprised him and, at the same time, had seemed to spark something within him. She picked up on the way his breathing had changed. Not only that, but the look in his eyes had darkened, making him look aroused, danger-ous...and oh, so tempting.

The mischievous side of her couldn't resist poking the bear even further to see how much control he had. Why not? Hadn't he planned to do the same thing to her? Test her con-trol, while having no intention of doing more than kissing her? Well, two could certainly play his game.

"Desiree?"

Why did he have to say her name in such a deep, sexy tone? "Yes?" He didn't say anything as he continued to stare at her. Was he going to tell her why he wouldn't take things beyond kissing? About his vow of celibacy?

Instead, he said, "The timing to do more isn't right for us now."

"Why not?" she asked again. She decided that if he didn't answer honestly this time, she wouldn't ask him again.

He didn't answer. Instead, he shifted closer, bringing his face just inches from hers. Before she could release her next breath, he captured her mouth with his.

CHAPTER 7

Cobra wasn't sure what he had expected when his lips touched Desiree's, but it hadn't been this—a sensual explosion that surged through his entire body. Nor had he expected his arms to immediately wrap around her and bring her closer to him as their tongues began tangling in a dance so sensuous, he heard himself moan. When had he ever moaned while kissing a woman?

But then, when had a woman's mouth fit so perfectly against his and tasted so damn sweet? Better than sweet, it tasted smoking hot. And why did he suddenly feel engulfed by a wave of heated emotions so intense, he couldn't shake them off, even if he wanted to.

He didn't.

He was too busy experiencing everything—her scent, her taste, just...her. It was like a high that he had never felt before. Their mouths were perfectly in sync, just like the fiery heat that seemed to be devouring them. At that moment, Cobra knew that he wanted this kiss to continue more than anything. He *needed* it.

He could feel the outline of her curvaceous body against his own, the feel of her breasts pressed against his chest, and her thighs cradling his. Every cell, molecule, and atom within him was in tune with the electrified mating of their mouths.

She suddenly pulled back, and he immediately felt a sense of loss. He stared at her, at her mouth swollen from his kisses, at her eyes, still glimmering with the combustible chemistry that had surged between them. Her scrumptious tongue had nearly been the death of him. And how he was watching her using that tongue to lick those gorgeous lips. Did she know that she was telling him that she'd liked his taste as much as he had hers?

"You got your kiss, Cobra. I hope you're satisfied."

If only she knew. During that period, while their mouths mated, he accepted that no amount of time with her would ever suffice. Point blank, he doubted he would ever get enough of her. And he didn't like the thought of that. He shifted his gaze from her mouth to her eyes—those beautiful hazel eyes that were still filled with heat.

"Oh, I'm immensely satisfied, Desiree." More than she knew and more than he had wanted. "And I look forward to kissing you again." However, he would not push his luck and try it again tonight. He had to pull himself together, reevaluate the situation, and revise his strategy. Because he'd discovered that Allison Desiree Sharpe was a woman who could hold her own.

"That won't be happening," she broke into his thoughts to say.

Cobra continued to stare at her, into eyes whose earlier heat now resembled chips of ice. Maybe it was time she knew where he stood. "The one thing you'll learn about me, Desiree, is that I love a good challenge. I'm going to make it my business to kiss you again—plenty of times, in fact—you will enjoy them as much as I will."

"You're too arrogant for your own good."

"And you taste too damn good for yours." He glanced at her desk and took a step back. "You're about ready to wrap up here?"

"Yes," she said, looking at him curiously before closing the manual she'd been reading. She was probably wondering how he could switch focus so easily. Little did she know that he hadn't actually. She was still the center of his attention.

"You look nice, today." She was wearing a royal blue pantsuit that made her look stylish and sophisticated.

"Thank you."

"You're welcome."

They turned out the lights as they left her office, then strolled silently side-by-side to the elevator. He wondered if, like him, she was thinking about their kiss. He had five more months of priming her to go, and was convinced the end result would be worth it. "What are your plans for the weekend?" he asked her.

She looked up at him as they waited for the elevator. "Why do you want to know?"

"Just curious."

She didn't say anything for a minute, then relented. "On Saturday, I tutor a group of adults who moved to this country and want to improve their English reading skills. And for some, their speaking skills as well."

"How did you become involved in something like that?"

"I heard the group was looking for volunteers. I thought it would be a good way to stay busy on weekends. So far, I have nothing planned for Sunday."

The elevator arrived, and they stepped inside. He tried not to notice how intimate being confined in such close quarters with her felt.

She glanced over at him. "What about you? Got big plans for the weekend?"

"I'm going home to Savannah. I have a second home there and often go back there to check on my family."

"All your family is there?"

"Not all. Only the older ones. Those in my generation moved away after college, but most still have second homes there. To stay close, we have a family reunion in Savannah every summer."

The elevator reached the bottom floor, and after saying goodnight to the men at the security desk, they stepped outside. He was glad he had managed to park right in front of the building.

"I envy you, Cobra."

He glanced at her as he opened the door for her. "Why?"

"There are advantages to having a big family," she said.

"And there are disadvantages. Everyone thinks they have the right to get into your business."

After snapping her seat belt in place, she pushed a lock of hair back from her face and looked at him. "Do you have family members who get into yours?"

He chuckled. "They try, but over the years, I've learned how to deal with it. I tell them what they need to know and nothing more." Before closing the door, he asked, "Are you comfortable?"

"Yes. This is a nice car."

"Thanks." He closed the door of his black Porsche Macan, then walked around to the front to get in on the other side.

***

Desiree watched him, her lips still tingling from the raw heat of his kiss. She had tried to downplay its impact on her senses, but it was damn near impossible. The man kissed as if he was branding her mouth to forever be his. As if he were learning every aspect of it, and hinting at the delights to come. His taste was still on her tongue, and his scent overwhelmed her. It seemed that after not engaging in any sexual activities—including kissing—for close to two years, every part of her had suddenly become revitalized. It was as if Cobra had somehow taken the genie out the bottle, and now, she was going to have a hard time getting it back in. She didn't like the thought of that.

As he moved around the car, it was like watching confidence in motion. Definitely a Barack Obama walk—relaxed and smooth. But with the perceptive way his head was aligned with his every step, she knew Cobra could claim it as his own. She would call it the *Cobra Sexy Stroll*.

When he opened the driver's door and slid onto the leather seat, she noticed how the denim material of his jeans stretched across a pair of taut thighs—thighs she'd felt against hers when they had kissed. Why was that fact so solidly rooted in her mind?

"You good?" he asked her.

She slid her gaze from his thighs and met his eyes. Had he caught her staring at him? "I'm good." Deciding that she would not let him get the best of her, she asked. "And what about you, Cobra? You good?"

A smile spread across his lips—a smile that could wet a woman's panties. "Desiree, after kissing you, I couldn't be better."

If his words were meant to stir her, trigger strong desires within her, then their kiss had already done that. However, she would keep that to herself.

Desiree glanced out the window as Cobra drove through the streets of New York, headed toward Harlem. The car was a smooth ride, and the red leather interior spoke not only of luxury but also high energy. "This car suits you."

He chuckled. "How so?"

She shrugged. He was conceited enough—she wasn't going to add to it, even if, like his car, he was beautifully built and moved with effortless elegance. Instead, she said, "It gives a good ride."

He brought the car to a traffic light and glanced over at her. She had deliberately said something she knew nothing about, but wanted to shake him up a bit, loosen some of his smooth control by making outlandish statements. Especially since she knew that he'd taken a vow of celibacy and could do nothing about it.

She met his gaze, and suddenly the car's interior felt heated. "And how do you know what kind of ride I give?" he asked.

"I don't. I'm just imagining what it would be like because of your personality and the image you project. But that doesn't mean I want to find out," she added quickly. Then, deciding to poke the bear again, she said, "Besides, I would hate for you to disappoint me."

"Did I disappoint you with my kiss, Desiree?"

She decided to be honest. "No."

"Trust me, I wouldn't disappoint you in the bedroom. I've never disappointed a woman I've spent time with. No real man would."

Aimery had. And he was rumored to be the hottest man on legs. "Let's just say I've experienced the opposite."

She looked away when she realized, a little too late, that she had given Cobra too much information.

"Trust me, Desiree, I don't doubt my skills in the bedroom. And I don't even have any doubts about yours."

She shrugged. Then, thinking she'd poked the bear enough for now, especially when she had revealed more about her personal business than she should have, she glanced out the car's window, appreciating the beauty of the night, as well as the silence between them.

When she'd first arrived in New York to live with her grandfather fourteen years ago, she'd moved into his place on the Sharpe Estate in Long Island. She loved the house because being there had reminded her of all the summer visits she'd had, when she was a child—to see her grandparents. Her grandfather had worked a lot back then, but the time Desiree had spent with her grandmother was still a special memory for her.

Desiree could vividly recall her grandmother, who had died when she'd been around ten. She remembered accompanying her parents to the funeral and how sad she had been knowing she would never see the kind and wonderful grandmother whose name she had been given.

She remembered Allison Sharpe as a stately, refined, and beautiful woman who always smiled and had a heart of gold. And during those summers, she'd also had plenty of love, time, and attention to give to a little girl who'd been neglected by her parents.

Those summers she'd spent in America had been the best times of her life. She'd felt loved and carefree. The Sharpes of Long Island had worked hard to project an image of a Black family worthy of admiration. They had worked hard, earned good educations, and achieved the American dream of a life of wealth, style, and honor.

They also lived by the family motto—'lifting while climbing'. Thanks to the Sharpe Family's support of numerous charities and their establishment of several scholarships, coordinated by her grandmother, the same opportunities and advantages that had been given to Richard and Allison Sharpe were shared with others. To this day, her grandfather remained a recognized philanthropist.

She had been proud to be named Allison, after the woman she had loved so very much. However, the summer before she was to leave for college, she'd come home from boarding school and discovered that her grandfather had decided to sell the house and buy a condo in Harlem, so he'd be closer to Manhattan.

Knowing that the most special times in her life—those wonderful and perfect summers she'd spent on the Sharpe Estate— would be lost to her forever, she made a radical decision—when she got to college, she told her friends to call her Desiree, not Allison.

Still, Desiree had to admit she had fallen in love with the luxury condo. It was spacious, and the wall-to-wall, floor-to-ceiling windows in the living room and dining room overlooked Central Park, Midtown, and the George Washington Bridge. The section of the condo she occupied opened onto a spectacular rooftop patio. After she returned from Paris, she'd assumed her grandfather would suggest that she get an apartment, but so far, he hadn't.

It helped that Helga, who had been the Sharpe's long-time cook and live-in housekeeper for years, was still with them. Richard Sharpe had purchased the older woman a smaller condo on the same floor in the building.

"You're home, Desiree."

Home. She glanced out of the windshield. Yes, she was home. Or at least, she considered the condo home...for now.

"Thanks for the ride, Cobra. I hope that you enjoy your time in Savannah with your family this weekend."

"I intend to," he said, parking the car.

"You don't have to park. I can go inside alone."

"You can withdraw your independent claws. I am a gentleman, and as one, I will be seeing you to the door." He got out of the car.

When he walked around and opened the door, she unsnapped her seat belt and took his hand, but not before he lightly stroked the racing pulse on her wrist. She released the sharp breath she was unable to suppress. From the smug look in his eyes, she knew his actions had been deliberate—he'd wanted to prove a point.

As she stepped out of the car, he didn't back up, and their bodies touched. "Remember what I said, Desiree. No woman has ever left my bed disappointed. Just something for you to think about..."

He finally took a step back, but kept her hand in his. When they reached the entrance where the doorman stood, she said to Cobra. "I'll be good from here."

"I'm walking you to your door."

She knew that she would be wasting her time arguing, so she nodded and walked beside him. For some reason, she appreciated the silence between them during the elevator ride.

When they reached her door, she turned to him. "Again, thanks, Cobra."

"No problem. I'm glad I showed up at your office. It was fun."

Before she could say anything, he leaned in and brushed a kiss across her lips. Knowing his intent, she decided to poke the bear again, and intentionally brushed her tongue across his lips.

What happened next was spontaneity at its best. He pulled her into his arms, and this kiss was even more passionate than the one in her office. It quickly deepened and became as hot and needy as she felt.

She might be poking him, but in return he was pushing her buttons in ways she hadn't counted on. This kiss just blew her away. Where before, he'd kissed her with wild, hungry abandonment, now, he was simply merciless. Every stroke of his tongue felt like he was marking her, leaving behind a signature she'd be forced to carry whether she wanted it or not.

Suddenly, he broke off the kiss and stared down at her. At that moment, she would have given anything to be able to read his thoughts, yet at the same time, she was very relieved that he couldn't read hers.

Reaching up, he slid his finger back and forth across her mouth, and whispered in a deep, husky voice. "If I'm not careful, Allison Desiree Sharpe, those lips of yours are going to be my downfall."

She could certainly say the same thing. Knowing she needed to get away from him quickly, if she was going to manage to take control of her heightened senses, she used her key to open the door, then turned back to him. "Goodnight, Cobra," she said, then quickly went inside.

***

As Cobra drove away from Richard's condo, he was stunned to realize that he had met his match with Desiree. But then, there was a good reason for it. He had met her at the most vulnerable time in his life. During one of his most sexually weak moments, when he was desperate for a physical connection—

in other words, desperate to get laid—and he was unable to move forward with it.

He still intended to prime her for what was to come, but for now, he figured the best thing to do would be to put distance between them. At least until he could reevaluate the situation and revise his strategy. That meant he would not deliberately seek her out again, like he had done tonight. If he happened to run into her on a Thursday night when he was playing chess with Richard, he would try like hell to control his urges where she was concerned.

It would be hard, but the only other option was to tell her about the bet with his brothers. And that was the last thing he wanted to do. Most women would assume that the thought of losing money was the underlying reason for his decision to keep his pants zipped, and that it was nothing more than a lack of self-control on his part. The last thing he wanted was to be seen as a man not in control of his emotions or physical urges.

The bet with his brothers was nothing more than motivation. After that episode with Bernice, sexual abstinence was something he would be doing regardless. The thought of taking his brothers' money in the process was simply icing on the cake. For him, it was about self-discipline. Not making love to a woman was a physical challenge he was determined to overcome.

He had to prove that he had the mental resilience and willpower to deny himself even the most seductive of temptations — like Desiree — if it meant maintaining absolute command over his desires and internal impulses. In other words, he would delay gratification for now to meet his long-term goal of never placing himself in a situation like the one he had with Bernice Whey ever again.

An hour later, he stood on the fourth-floor rooftop of his brownstone. If he looked past a bunch of trees and a couple of buildings, he could see the condo where the Sharpes lived. Why did he still have Desiree on his mind? Why was he still remembering every moment he'd spent with her tonight? Had she actually hinted that she and a former lover had been sexually incompatible in the bedroom? Was that why she thought they might be as well? Well, he couldn't wait to prove differently. He had no doubt the two of them would light the bedsheets on fire.

When his phone rang, he pulled it from the pocket of his jeans. He knew who it was on the line. His friend Anthony Tombstone. "What's up, Tomb?"

"You're still coming home this weekend?"

"Yes."

"Then we can celebrate?"

Cobra lifted a brow. "Celebrate what?"

"You will have made it through eight months of celibacy, with only four more to go. Just so you know, I got my money on you."

Cobra frowned. "And who are you betting with?"

"Straw. He doesn't think you can do it."

"Oh, he doesn't, does he?"

"Nope. And we need to prove him wrong. I have two hundred dollars riding on you, and I don't want to lose my money, Cobra."

"You won't," he assured Tomb.

"Good."

"I'll see you Saturday, and we can celebrate at any place but Swanky's," Cobra said. Swanky's had always been his 'go to' nightclub whenever he came home to visit, but not anymore. He hadn't set foot in the place since the night he met Bernice Whey there.

"I hear you," Tomb said, chuckling.

After ending the call with Tombstone, and being reminded of that fateful night when he almost lost everything, Cobra was more determined than ever not to be tempted by Allison Desiree Sharpe.

***

"I'm glad the play went well, Camille. And I just saw the reviews! Fantastic! But why are you up so early? It's eleven o'clock in New York, which means it's five in the morning there," Desiree said, shifting to a good position in bed.

"I didn't sleep much after the play. I was too hyped up. You know how it is with me on the final night. The place was packed. Today is Friday, so there aren't any clinicals. I get to hang around the flat and make this a 'do nothing' day."

"I wish I could do the same. I have to report for work at eight."

"How are things going with that, Rae?"

"So far so good. I'm really enjoying myself just learning the different jobs. The executive team is awesome and like Granddad, they are surprised that I know so much about business, considering I graduated from a liberal arts school."

"I guess that means you haven't told your grandfather what you were doing the past three years?"

"No, not yet. I'm waiting for the right time."

"And how is your relationship with him going?" Camille asked.

Desiree released a deep sigh. "I'm not sure, Cam. He's usually gone when I get up in the morning. However, I've been working late the past few days, and he doesn't retire for the night until he knows I'm home. But he always did that whenever I came home from school."

"So, what's different?"

"He appears more at peace somehow. Whenever we share a meal, he seems genuinely interested in how my day went or how things are going at the office. I think he's confused since I've yet to go to a nightclub. At the office, everyone knows I'm Richard Sharpe's granddaughter, so of course, they treat me with respect. But it's obvious they have high expectations for me."

"Does that bother you?"

"Not at all. I'm more like my grandfather than my father in that regard. I love being a part of corporate America and the challenges it presents. My dad, on the other hand, detested it. I think he would have much preferred to be part of the philanthropic arm of the Sharpe Corporation, as my grandmother was. Dad was always more interested in the social obligations of the company, and he would have been better suited to attending galas, speaking at events, and maintaining the family's public image or reputation."

"I concur with that," Camille said. "I always thought your father's alcoholism might have stemmed from the pressure of being put in a job where he was expected to follow in his father's footsteps. I think deep down, he knew that he would never measure up to it."

Desiree agreed with her friend's psychological assessment of Richard Sharpe, Jr. "I think it's important to learn the best of both business worlds. I have always admired my grandmother and the role she played in helping to build and sustain the Sharpe's dynasty. However, I also want to learn the corporation's core business strategies. And I don't know of a better person to teach me than Granddad."

"How are things between you and Cobra Masters after your blow-up earlier this week?"

Desiree shifted on her back to stare up at the ceiling. Her mouth was still tingling from the kisses they'd shared. "Would you believe that he showed up at the office tonight. Unannounced."

"Why?"

"To take me home." She then told Camille everything.

"Sounds like Cobra Masters is one *hot tamale*, as Melia would say."

Emelia Sellers had moved into their apartment building when she'd been attending an art school in Paris. She, Camille, and Desiree had instantly hit it off and become good friends. Desiree had often heard Melia use that term to describe any handsome, hot-blooded man who captured her attention. Melia was from the Mississippi Delta, where the '*hot tamale*' description was commonly used, though it usually referred to spicy food rather than the opposite sex.

"He is definitely that. At least I don't have to worry about him wanting to go beyond kisses."

"Why not?"

Desiree told Camille what she had heard in the ladies' room earlier in the week.

"Wow, Rae. Can you imagine how that woman could have destroyed Cobra Masters' life and career? I'm glad he managed to catch her in the act. It must have been quite a night!"

"I'm glad he caught her, too. Although I don't like Cobra, I wouldn't wish such a thing on my worst enemy."

"Hmmm... You still want to claim that you don't like him...even after you let him kiss you?"

"I don't see why that's so strange. He deliberately kissed me until I got all hot and bothered, all the time knowing that he wouldn't do anything about it. That shows just what a manipulator he is."

"Would you have let him do something about it?"

"No, and you know why." Her best friend knew her history with men.

"Yes, I do, so what's the problem? Is it that you feel he should have confided in you about his celibacy? If so, why? It's a private matter, and most men wouldn't want such a thing exposed. Especially to a woman he might be attracted to."

"If our roles were reversed, I would have no problem letting him know my situation," Desiree said.

"Would you? Need I remind you that you *are* in that situation, Rae? Not for the same reason, since your decision to abstain from sex is self-imposed, thanks to that asshole Aimery. Still, women in general have no problem establishing boundaries while they're building an emotional connection with a man. But men don't think the same way. They tend to think with the wrong head, and it gets them into all kinds of trouble. I'm not excusing them—trust me—but that's the way it is for them."

Desiree knew she should listen to Camille's advice. She hadn't graduated at the top of her psychology studies for nothing. But still... "Then Cobra shouldn't kiss me into making me want more, Cam. Especially when he has no intention of delivering. If a woman did such a thing, she'd be accused of being a tease." She sighed, then added wistfully, "His kisses were so hot, they reminded me of how long it's been since I slept with a man."

Camille didn't say anything for a minute, then finally added in a soft voice, "But think what those same hot kisses were doing to him, Rae. He's not immune. After what that woman tried to do to him, I can understand why he'd put sex on the back burner for a while, just like I understood your reasons for doing the same thing after Aimery. Still, I'm sure it has to be hard for a man like Cobra, whose sexual escapades are the stuff of legends."

"Well, I'm not letting him use me to appease his sexual hunger," Desiree declared vehemently.

"Hmmm, did you ever think that maybe he just likes kissing you? And I think you enjoyed kissing him, too. Sounds like temptation is getting the best of you, and you're rethinking your own decision not to get involved with anyone, Rae."

"Even if I were rethinking my decision, Cobra is in no position to do anything about it."

Camille didn't say anything for a moment and then said, "Although you know about his vow of celibacy, he knows nothing about your situation, right? What are the odds that you two are in the exact same predicament?"

"Well, just to be on the safe side, I've decided to stay out of his way and start avoiding him as much as I can. When he comes over on Thursday nights to play chess with Granddad, I'll make sure that I'm not here."

"Do whatever you think you have to. But for now, go to sleep, Rae. You have to get up early in the morning."

"I will. But I just want to say one more thing. I noticed you didn't mention anything about Léandre."

"There's nothing to tell. Although he hasn't said anything to me about it, Kassie mentioned tonight that, now that the production has ended, Léandre is thinking about taking a few weeks off to work on a new script. He's going to be spending that time in a place in the Swiss Alps."

Kassie, Léandre's sister, often helped on the production set.

"The Swiss Alps?" Desiree asked.

"Yes. A friend of his offered him the use of his Swiss mountain cabin. I guess he didn't think it was important enough to mention it to me."

Desiree could hear the hurt in her best friend's voice. "I still think you should just come out and tell him how you feel, Cam."

"I'm not ready to do that, Rae. What if he doesn't feel the same way about me that I feel about him?"

"You'll never know if you don't act on it."

"I know... Well, goodnight, Rae."

"Goodnight, Cam."

After hanging up the phone, Desiree thought about how much, and for how long, Camille had loved Léandre. All the way back when the two were in high school. That was a long time for a girl to wait for the boy of her dreams to notice her as more than a friend. Hopefully, one day Léandre would finally open his eyes.

CHAPTER 8

"So, when are you leaving?" Cobra asked Richard when they had finished their chess game. This was one of the rare times that he had actually won. When Richard mentioned his plans, Cobra understood why the man hadn't been as focused tonight.

"First thing in the morning. I'm looking forward to seeing Lolita and meeting her daughter, son-in-law, and her newest grandbaby."

Cobra nodded. "How long will you be gone?"

"Three weeks."

When Cobra started to rise to put on his jacket and leave, Richard said, "There's a favor I need to ask of you. It's regarding Allison."

Cobra eased back in his chair. He had a feeling he would not like whatever favor Richard was about to ask of him. Four weeks had passed since the night he and Desiree had kissed. The last three Thursdays when he'd come over to play chess with Richard, Desiree had been working late. Tonight, he had been pleasantly surprised when she had joined him and Richard for dinner. But she had little to say and left soon after to go out.

"How can I help you?"

"I'll be gone for a while, and I want to make sure Allison has someone she can call if something comes up. If it's okay with you, I want to leave your contact information with her."

Cobra figured that even if Richard were to give her the information, hell would likely freeze over before she used it. "You can certainly do that, Richard."

"Thanks. And I haven't mentioned anything about Lolita to Desiree yet. I plan on talking to her when I return. She assumes I'm going out of town on a business trip to check on my two international offices."

Cobra nodded again. "That sounds like a plan." He stood to reach for his jacket, then slid into it. "Just wondering... Where did Desiree run off to in a hurry?"

Richard began putting the chess game away. "I believe she said she was going ice skating."

"Ice skating?"

"Yes. There's an ice-skating rink on the amenity floor."

"She went alone?" Cobra asked.

"She didn't say." Richard finished putting the game away, then looked up at Cobra. "I had a meeting with Saul Lawrence today. He told me something rather interesting."

Saul Lawrence was Richard's second-in-command and had been among the first people Richard hired when he started the company years ago.

"And what did Lawrence have to say?" Cobra asked.

"It seems that Allison is very knowledgeable about business. After her cross-training in various positions within the company, she put together a detailed written report on ways to streamline a number of them for efficiency, while at the same time not eliminating anyone's job."

"That's impressive," Cobra said.

"Saul thought so, too. He claims her keen sense of intelligence on business matters reminds him of me."

Cobra chuckled. "You sound surprised. Why? She is, after all, your granddaughter."

Richard leaned back in his chair. "I believe that I made a number of mistakes where Allison is concerned."

Cobra heard the despondency in his voice and slid back down in the chair. "How so?"

"I lost my son just two years after I lost my wife. Grief compounded on grief. A part of me thinks I should have given in to Allison's aunt's request for full custody of her at the time. But I refused. After losing my wife and son, I didn't want to lose my granddaughter, too. However, when Allison arrived, I didn't know what to do with her. I could see that she was hurting. It was understandable—she'd just lost both her parents. Still, it was hard enough for me to deal with my own grief, and I couldn't take on hers."

"Is that why you shipped her off to a boarding school?"

Richard went silent for a moment, then asked. "She told you about that?"

"Yes. At the wedding reception, when we danced. I think she took it as rejection. Is she right, Richard?"

"No. Absolutely not. However, I can see why Allison would assume that." He shook his head slowly. "The truth is that I loved her too much to let her get close. I was terrified I'd lose her the same way I lost the others."

Cobra got to his feet again. "You want to know what I think, Richard?"

"Not really."

Cobra grinned. "You never do, yet as always, I'm going to tell you anyway. It's obvious that you and Desiree have issues to resolve. Deep issues. And I honestly think you should try to resolve them before you introduce her to Lolita. Desiree is not a child. If you were to tell her what you just told me, I think she'd understand. And if she doesn't, at least you'd have tried to explain things to her."

Cobra paused and then added, "You need to get to know your granddaughter, Richard. Saul isn't wrong. During the infrequent times I've been around Desiree, I've seen a lot in her character that reminds me of you. Remember how distrustful you were in the beginning? You always had your guard up, as if you weren't certain who you should allow yourself to get close. Well, I've seen that same personality trait in Desiree. The two of you aren't as different as you think."

Cobra paused to let what he'd just said sink in. "And those outlandish things she might have done in the past? Maybe it was her way to get your attention." He moved over to stand by Richard's side. "Enjoy your trip. You can leave knowing that if Desiree needs anything, I'll be there for her."

Cobra walked to the door, then turned and asked, "Your owners' code to the amenity floor is still the same?"

"Yes."

He nodded, appreciating that Richard hadn't asked why he'd wanted to know. "Good night, Richard. Say hi to Lolita for me."

He nodded. "I will. Good night. I'll see you when I return."

***

Desiree smiled as she twirled around on the ice, realizing how much she'd missed this. She had had her first figure skating lesson when she'd been only four, with dreams of one day becoming a member of the Paris Figure Skating Olympic Team like her Aunt Margot.

Although it was the end of July, the huge room where the ice rink was located was cold. Still, that hadn't stopped her from putting on the figure skating outfit her aunt had given her for her eighteenth birthday. Even her skates had been a gift from her aunt.

Her cell phone was blasting Wind Beneath My Wings. It was the perfect skating soundtrack—slow, emotional—and it allowed her to try out a series of moves that she hadn't performed in years.

A few minutes in, she was happy to realize that she hadn't lost any of her skills on the ice. She'd heard that some things just stayed with a person, becoming a part of them. And for her, figure skating had been that. It was an important thing that she and her aunt had shared.

As she moved around the rink, gliding over the ice, she skated to the center and closed her eyes as the music settled into her mind, going straight to her soul. She did a few swizzles, dips, and two-foot glides to find the balance she needed. Then she progressed to more challenging moves, including a double axel, twirling in the air before landing perfectly.

Then she was gliding over the ice again, performing another jump. As the song came to an end, she twirled directly into a fast spin and finally a slow bow.

It was only when the music stopped that she realized she wasn't alone. Her heart rate increased as she lifted her head to glance around the rink. Then she saw him. Cobra was standing on the sidelines, leaning against the rail. And he was staring at her.

***

Cobra had never seen movements so graceful, so perfectly timed, and executed in a way that had held him spellbound. He hadn't been concentrating on that very short, nearly backless figure skating outfit she wore that barely touched her thighs and emphasized her lush curves—and that surprised him. Because she was a sight he'd never forget.

But what had really held his attention was the way she had glided across the ice, how her entire body had been in sync with every twirl, spin, and bow. And the way her hair had flowed around her shoulders while executing the different maneuvers had made him long to run his hands through it.

Even from a distance, he saw her frown and the tightening of her lips. She was probably wondering what he was doing here. In truth, he was wondering the same thing himself. The moment he had stepped on the elevator, he couldn't resist pressing the button for the eighth floor instead of the main one. Richard had told him she was skating, and that should have been his cue to go home for the evening. But he couldn't stop himself from seeing her in action, and now that he was here, he couldn't take his eyes off of her.

She skated over to him. "Cobra."

"Desiree."

"What are you doing here?"

"You ran off after dinner."

She lifted a brow. "Was I supposed to hang around or something?"

He shoved his hands into the pockets of his slacks. "I guess not. You looked good out there. I take it you've had lessons."

"Yes. From the time I was four," she said, letting her guard down a little. "I don't skate as much as I used to, and I miss it. Tonight I decided to dress the part and run through a few routines."

"Well, I'm impressed. You're a wonderful skater." And that was an understatement. Her body had personified sensuality in motion. Each movement had been flawless. And when she had spun around at the end, she'd stolen his breath away.

"When I was young, I'd dreamed of being on France's Olympic figure skating team. Then my parents died, and I came to the States."

"Did you stop your lessons?" he asked her.

"No. Granddad promised Aunt Margot, who was on the Olympic team when she was younger, that I would continue my lessons. He signed me up for them at boarding school."

"So, why didn't you try out for the US team?"

She pushed a lock of hair back from her face, making him even more aware of her stunning facial features, especially the beauty of her eyes. "I would have felt like a traitor. After all, I learned everything about it in Paris." She shook her head. "You still haven't told me why you're here. Who gave you the passcode to get off on this floor?"

"You ran off so quickly after dinner. I wanted to make sure you were okay. You're here all alone. I was worried." For an unclear reason, he had developed a protective instinct toward her.

But there was another reason he'd sought her out. He had gone almost four weeks without interacting with her. He had to admit, avoidance had taken the edge off his horniness somewhat. And flying out to LA last week to spend some time with his nephew also helped. However, being in Desiree's presence during dinner—although for less than an hour—had changed things. Just sharing space with her had immediately sent his libido into overdrive.

Sitting across the table, he'd had a good view of her, and he'd been close enough to be enveloped in her sensual scent. She barely looked at him, but he hadn't been able to keep his eyes off her. He was glad Richard had carried most of the conversation, with him and Desiree responding only when prompted.

"Well, as you can see, I'm alone but fine. And I happen to enjoy my privacy, so there's nothing to worry about. Feel free to leave," she said, dropping onto one of the rink-side benches to remove her skates.

Not ready to leave just yet, he slid onto the bench beside her. She looked up and glared at him. "Do you mind?"

"Do I mind what?" he asked.

"Could you give me some alone time?"

It was on the tip of his tongue to tell her he'd already done that. For four whole weeks, he'd avoided her. This weekend would mark a successful nine months of celibacy, with only three more to go. That was almost historic. "I'd prefer to spend some time with you, Desiree."

"Oh? Is that why you've avoided me for nearly four weeks?"

He could tell by the way she suddenly returned to the task of removing her skates that she hadn't meant to ask that question. It would appear that she had been bothered by his absence. "Do you miss me not coming to the office to take you home, Desiree?"

"Of course not!" she said with indignation.

"Then what's the issue? I haven't changed my schedule since you moved back to New York. I still play chess with

Richard every Thursday night at the condo where you live. So, it seems to me that you're the one doing the avoiding."

"I have no reason to avoid you, Cobra. You're the one who wanted to kiss me that night. I was just a bystander."

Her words hit a nerve because, yes, he had wanted that kiss. Desperately so. And although he should have regretted their encounter, he didn't. Memories of that kiss were what had kept him sane for the past four weeks. Even now, just looking at her mouth was gripping his gut because he wanted to taste her as he'd done before.

"What about you, Desiree? Do you ever think about that kiss?" he asked, trying like hell to keep his gaze on her face and not let it dip to her chest. He lost the battle, and nearly swallowed his tongue when he saw her hardened nipples pressing through the fabric of her outfit. Didn't she know that was one of the signs of an aroused woman? Damn, he wished he didn't.

"I can barely remember it," she said lightly as she stood.

He stood as well, and their bodies brushed against each other. His breath caught in his throat, and his gaze moved to her lips. She was so close... But he couldn't. Could he?

"Prove it," he said, in a voice so deep he almost couldn't recognize it as his own. What was wrong with him? Why was this woman, of all the women he'd been with, driving him so insane? Why was he so drawn to her? He again blamed it on his celibate state. That had to be it. If he had been spending time with other women, he wouldn't be giving Desiree a second thought. Of course, he knew that was a lie the moment the notion flashed through his mind.

When their lips were mere inches apart, she whispered, "Like I said, Cobra, you were the one who wanted to kiss me that night. The same way you want to kiss me right now."

Because of that damn bet with his brothers, he knew the dangers he faced each time he and Desiree kissed. The temptation, the allure, the desire for more. However, he knew there was a reason he wanted to be so close to her, even now, though it was driving him mad. He was priming her for what was to come.

Satisfied with that reasoning, he captured her mouth, needing the feel of it, and more importantly, the taste. When she released a soft moan, he dug in, kissing her for all it was worth, and in his book, that was plenty.

***

Over the past weeks, Desiree had managed to convince herself that she didn't want to see Cobra, yet tonight, she hadn't been able to stay away, and had decided to dine with him and her grandfather. Although she had done her best to ignore him during the meal, she had felt the heat of his gaze each and every time he had looked across the table at her. It had been like a heated caress, touching her entire body. And those times when he had responded to something her grandfather had said, the deep, husky sound of his voice had stroked something inside her. It felt like a warm blanket settling over her—a blanket she would love to cuddle beneath with him.

That was the reason she hadn't wasted any time leaving the condo after dinner, coming here to skate out all the emotions she hadn't wanted to feel but did. Why was she letting Cobra get under her skin? Or maybe a better question to ask was why she was now letting him devour her mouth as if he owned it?

She knew she should end this madness now, but his mouth tasted too hot, too delectable, yet somehow soothing.

For years, skating had been her solace, but his kisses offered her a refuge she'd never found on the ice.

A warning inside her head told her she should pull back, end the kiss now, but she couldn't. She wanted more, and couldn't resist reaching out to wrap her arms around his neck, holding tight while mimicking each thrust of his tongue. He was aroused. Deeply aroused. She could feel the hardness of him press into her, and she shifted to cradle his erection between her parted thighs. She heard his guttural groan, and when he placed his hands on her backside to press her closer to him, she let out a groan of her own.

"The skating rink will close in five minutes," a loud voice boomed over the intercom, interrupting at the worst possible moment.

She pulled back to end the kiss when it seemed Cobra had no intention of doing so. "I guess it's time to leave," she whispered against his moist lips.

"Yeah, I guess so," Cobra responded, in what sounded like a grumble.

She pulled her cover-up from her gym bag and put it on over her head, then adjusted it so it fell just above her knees. "I'm ready."

He grabbed her gym bag off the bench. After putting the straps over his shoulder, he reached for her hand. "Then let's go."

Nodding at the older man who stood by the rink's door, they left, trying not to act embarrassed at the thought they had been caught kissing. At least, that was what she was doing, but she knew a blush stained her cheeks all the same.

They walked silently toward the elevator, hand in hand. Needing to regain some semblance of control of the situation, she glanced over at Cobra and asked, "So who won chess?"

He smiled. "I did. Richard wasn't focused tonight."

She nodded. "I bet that doesn't happen very often."

"No, it doesn't."

***

Cobra inwardly cursed at the man's untimely interruption of their kiss, although he should have welcomed it. Damn. He had been less than a minute from unlocking his zipper and easing Desiree down on that bench and...

"Cobra, you never told me how you got access to this floor. It's only for tenants."

"Yeah, that's true. Unless you're a guest of one of those residents, who happens to share their passcode with you. The racquetball court is also on this floor, as well as several other sports amenities that I get to enjoy, thanks to your grandfather."

"Lucky you."

"Yes, lucky me." *Lucky that she was leaving it at that.*

When they reached the elevator, he pressed the button. Once inside the enclosed quarters, they could finish the kiss they started in the rink, though that wasn't a good idea. From her demeanor, Cobra could tell she was already putting distance between them again. The last time he was all for it, but after nearly a month, he decided he needed to take a different approach with Desiree. The less that he saw of her, the more he wanted her. It was a problem.

He glanced over at her, glad she had put on a cover-up. He couldn't imagine the looks she would have received if they'd run into anyone while she was wearing that sexy ice-skating outfit. Still, even covered up, she looked smoking hot. "So... Do you have any plans for the weekend, Desiree?"

"And you want to know, why?"

He was getting used to her smart mouth. However, he doubted whether he would get used to tasting it. "Just curious."

She didn't say anything for a minute, as if wondering if she should answer his question, then admitted, "Saturday morning, I'm teaching that reading class again."

"And Saturday night?" Cobra knew better than to ask if she would be going to a nightclub. He'd discovered that her history as a party girl was a touchy subject with her.

"Not sure. Why?"

"How do you feel about attending a Broadway play with me?"

She looked at him with surprise. "You're asking me out on a date?"

"Yes. Why not? Since you think I have ulterior motives regarding Richard, this will give you a chance to get to know me better."

"And what if I said that I don't want to get to know you better?"

"That would be unfair. Especially after what you accused me of."

The elevator arrived, and they stepped inside. The door slid closed after he pressed the button for her floor. She seemed to think about his question. Finally, she said, "Okay, Cobra, I'll go out with you Saturday night, as long as you don't try any funny business."

Try any funny business? There wasn't anything amusing about kissing her, and that was all he could do because of that damn bet. He'd been serious as hell while devouring her mouth, trying to kiss the taste off her lips. But if she needed reassurance... "I promise I won't try any funny business, Desiree."

When the elevator door opened on her floor, she stepped out and didn't pull her hand from his until they stood in front of her condo. He then took her gym bag from his shoulder and handed it to her. "Thanks."

"You're welcome. And I need your number."

She lifted a brow. "My number?"

"Yes, your phone number in case I get delayed picking you up on Saturday," he said, pulling out his phone.

She nodded and rattled off her phone number to him. "Good night, Cobra." When she turned to unlock the door to her condo, he reached and pulled her to him.

"I want to leave you with something to remember. Think about me until we see each other Saturday," he whispered.

He then sealed his lips over hers, wanting this kiss to have a different kind of punch than the others they'd shared. There was no game playing, no red flags going off in his head, and no manipulative intention. For this kiss, he wanted a genuine connection to her. For a reason he couldn't explain, he needed it.

CHAPTER 9

At the sound of the doorbell, Desiree took a quick glance in the full-length mirror, then grabbed her purse and jacket from her bed. Yesterday, she had been so close to calling Cobra to tell him that she had changed her mind about tonight. The kiss he'd left her with Thursday night told her a truth she couldn't ignore: he was completely out of her league.

No matter how many times she had brushed her teeth, she could still taste him. And as much as she didn't want to admit it, she rather liked the flavor. He had said he wanted to leave her with something to remember until they saw each other again, and he had certainly succeeded in doing that.

She opened the door and saw him standing there, exuding effortless charm in dark, tailored slacks and a crisp white button-down, with a jacket casually draped over his arm. Why did he have to look so damn good? "Hello, Cobra."

His gaze slid over her from top to bottom. "Desiree, you look great."

"Thanks," she replied, glad for the extra time and attention she had given to her hair and makeup. The dress she was wearing was one she had purchased in Paris at a boutique she normally frequented. Camille had been with her when she'd found it and had told her that it looked fantastic. She'd counted on that when she'd decided to wear it tonight.

She stepped out in the corridor and closed the door behind her. Helga had the weekends off, and without her grandfather's presence, the condo had felt very empty.

"The show doesn't start until nine. That will give us time to grab something to eat first. I know this great restaurant in Times Square."

She glanced at him as they headed toward the elevator. "You didn't mention anything about dinner."

He met her gaze. "Merely an oversight. Have you eaten already?"

"No."

"Good. Have you ever eaten at Lucki Pond?"

She had heard people rave about the upscale Manhattan restaurant known for its fine dining. "No, I haven't."

"Then tonight you're in for a treat. It's one of my favorite places," he said as they stepped on the elevator. "You won't be disappointed."

Desiree nodded as the elevator door closed. "I'll take your word for it."

An hour later, she had to admit that Cobra was right. Eating dinner at the Lucki Pond had been a treat. He told her he loved pork chops as he ordered the Pork Marsala with mushrooms and asparagus. Following his lead, she had done the same, and she hadn't been disappointed. For dessert, he had chosen a strawberry cheesecake, and she had ordered a chocolate mousse cake.

Knowing that, in life as well as in business, it was important to understand an adversary, she said, "Tell me about your family, Cobra."

Her question made him look up from his dessert. His dark eyes appraised her, and she could actually feel heat emitting from them.

"What do you want to know, Desiree?"

"Whatever you want to tell me."

He took a sip of his wine and then said, "As you know, I'm a triplet, the youngest one. Cortez is seven minutes older than Colton and fifteen minutes older than me." He chuckled. "Dad claimed he nearly got drunk that night. He and Mom thought they were only having twins. The doctor said I'd been lying low, lurking in the shadows like a snake. That's why Dad decided to name me Cobra."

He paused for a moment, then continued. "My parents are still alive and well. They were childhood sweethearts who got married after college, and who, to this day, still love each other deeply. There was never a time we didn't know the strength of our parents' love. And we always knew that we were a product of that love."

Cobra placed his fork down. "We had a health scare with Dad a few years back."

She lifted a brow. "What happened?"

"He had a heart attack. We were all away from home, in college, and he wasn't taking care of himself—working long hours, eating whatever he wanted, and not being active. Luckily, he survived and was forced to change his lifestyle and eating habits. Mom, my brothers, and I did, as well. As a family, we all decided to take better care of ourselves."

She nodded as she eased a slice of cake into her mouth. That had to have been scary for them. She had met his parents at Colton's wedding. Her grandfather had introduced them to her. She would never have guessed that Mr. Masters had had a heart attack. He'd seemed in good physical shape. Suddenly, she remembered something Cobra had said. "*...I try to encourage Richard to stay active and eat healthy in order to live longer.*"

Now she knew that what had happened to his father likely had more bearing on why he took such an interest in her grandfather's physical well-being. She shook her head slightly. It obviously had nothing at all to do with what she had accused him of.

"What about your grandparents? Are they still alive?" she asked, wanting to change the subject.

"No. My grandmother died within months of my grandfather."

"My goodness. She probably couldn't go on without him."

Cobra chuckled. "That wasn't the case at all. Granddad had been married five times, and Granny three. She was his fourth wife, and he had been her third husband. However, they did maintain a good friendship until the end."

His words made her curious. "What do you mean?"

"After divorcing wife number five, Granddad Kenneth moved back into the neighborhood. In fact, his place was only a few doors down from where my grandmother lived."

"You don't think he was trying to get back with her?"

"No. That ship had sailed. He had been unfaithful, and my grandmother was unforgiving. But Granddad Kenneth wanted to be near his sons, grandchildren, and great-grandchildren. He said that moving so close to where my grandmother lived made it easier on everyone. We could visit him whenever we visited our granny. I admit it was nice going from one house to the other without leaving the street. Granny was the only one of his wives who gave him kids. Or, at least, that's what we had thought for years."

"He had other kids?"

"Just one. From his first wife. A son that Granddad Kenneth died not knowing about. We only learned about that particular Masters last year."

"How?" If he thought she was diving too deep into his family's personal business, he wasn't saying.

"His first marriage only lasted six months, but when she left, she was pregnant. The baby was born seven months after they divorced. For reasons we have yet to understand, she decided not to ever tell him about it."

He took another sip of his wine. "Last year, my cousin Quinn got a call from social services in Philadelphia. A twelve-year-old boy named Hayes Masters' parents had been killed when the store they owned was robbed. Hayes is Kenneth's great-grandson from his first wife. Her son, Isley, was the child she'd hidden from Kenneth. None of us knew Isley, or anything about his son Sonny. But at least we're getting to know Hayes."

"Where is the boy now?"

After picking his fork back up and sliding the last piece of cake into his mouth, Cobra leaned back in his chair. "He's with Quinn and Alexia."

She knew Quinn Masters was a well-known entertainment attorney in LA and was married to Grammy Award-winning artist, Alexia Bennett Masters. She had met them at Colton and Kelly's wedding. "Is he okay?"

"He is, though there was a long adjustment period. After all, he'd just lost both his parents. But thanks to Alexia and Quinn, he's on the right track. The entire Masters family came together to let him know he was one of us and that we would always be there for him."

Desiree nodded. The boy's situation hit a little too close to home. She would have loved to hear something like that from her grandfather when he'd become her guardian. "I'm glad. I love happy endings."

***

A few hours later, Cobra walked her to her door. "Did you enjoy the play?" he asked.

"Oh yes! I've always wanted to see The Lion King. Thanks for such a wonderful evening."

"You're very welcome. So, what are your plans for tomorrow?" he asked.

"I'm taking tomorrow off and just relaxing. I'm going to sleep late, then maybe do some shopping. What about you?"

"Unlike you, I have to get up early. I'm playing tennis with a college friend who recently moved to Brooklyn. He loves the game, so we agreed to meet in the morning to get a few matches in before the day starts. Then that afternoon, I have a Zoom call with my family. I'm on the committee that's hosting our family reunion next weekend."

"A family reunion sounds like fun."

"It always is when the Masters get together."

They stopped at her door, and she turned to him. Anticipation was running through her. He had never walked her to the door without kissing her, and she saw no reason tonight would be any different. She had enjoyed dinner and the play, and he had been a perfect gentleman. He'd kept his word and hadn't tried any funny business.

"Thanks again for tonight, Cobra."

"It was my pleasure."

She didn't want it to seem like she was expecting him to kiss her, but when he took a step toward her, she took one toward him. But instead of pulling her into his arms, he asked in a low voice. "Aren't you going to invite me in, Desiree?"

Invite him in? He had to be kidding. "Why would I do that?"

He reached up and lightly traced her lips with the thumb of his finger, making all sorts of tingling sensations erupt in her stomach. "Usually, that's how an evening ends. You invite your date in for something to drink—beer, coffee, wine, or even water."

Leaning in close, he whispered, "However, I do have another reason for wanting you to invite me inside."

Desiree caught herself before she got too excited. He wouldn't do anything that would make him lose the bet he'd made with his brothers. So what was he doing? "And what reason is that?"

So, I can give you the kind of kiss you deserve."

***

To her credit, Desiree remained composed despite suddenly feeling incredibly hot inside. Just what kind of kiss did he think she deserved? Those women who'd boasted of his bedroom skills were probably right. After all, she'd only been on the receiving end of Cobra's kisses, but she knew he was truly a master. His kisses had made any she'd experienced before seem like childish pecks. Because Cobra hadn't just kissed her, he'd drunk in the very breath from her lungs. It was as if her lips had been the only sustenance he'd needed, and he'd claimed every inch of her mouth with a desperation that she'd felt through her whole body. Did he think that hadn't been mind-blowing enough for her? That she deserved another kind of kiss? For crying out loud, just what did he have in mind? She might be playing with fire, but she wanted to find out.

"Cobra?"

He stared at her with those intense dark eyes. "Yes, Desiree?"

"Would you like to join me in a glass of wine before leaving?" she asked, trying to calm the anticipation that was flowing all through her.

"I would love to."

She unlocked the door, and he followed her inside.

CHAPTER 10

"**W**ould you prefer red or white wine, Cobra?"

He glanced over at Desiree, who'd run her tongue over her bottom lip. She was nervous. That much was obvious. "I try to watch my intake of wine, and since I had a glass at dinner, I'd prefer a cup of coffee if it won't be any trouble."

"It won't. How do you like it?"

"Black."

She nodded. "Alright. I'll be back in a minute."

He watched her walk off toward the kitchen, admiring her as she went. She looked great tonight. That little black dress accentuated all her curves and made her legs look like they'd go on forever. And he liked her hair tonight, too. The way it was pinned up on her head showcased the gracefulness and beauty of her neck. When had he ever become aroused from seeing a woman's neck before? He rubbed his hand down his face, questioning the wisdom of being alone in this condo with her.

Because of what he'd said before coming in, she likely assumed he would pull her into his arms and kiss her the moment they were behind closed doors. But for him, giving her the kiss she deserved included cherishing both the moment itself and building the slow anticipation up to it. He wanted their kiss to be so much more than just a fleeting moment, a preplanned action. He wanted to relish the journey as much as the destination.

Removing his jacket, he placed it across the back of the sofa, then walked over to the window. Richard preferred to keep the curtains open so he could fully enjoy the unobstructed view of Central Park, Midtown, and the George Washington Bridge.

He was glad he'd ordered a luxury sedan instead of driving his own car tonight. It was a weekend, after all, and he had anticipated heavy traffic. However, ordering the sedan had one drawback, and he realized it immediately when he had slid into the backseat beside Desiree. Her intoxicating scent had filled the car's interior, and his erection had immediately responded.

Dinner, too, had been a challenge. His attention had been solely on her mouth, while his imagination wandered, thinking about all the things he wanted to do to it and with it.

"Here you are, Cobra."

He turned and watched as she placed the cup and saucer on the sofa table, noting only one. "You're not joining me?"

"Drinking coffee this late will interfere with my sleep."

Leaving his place by the window, he crossed to the table, picked up the coffee cup, took a couple of sips, and looked at her. She had moved to sit in a chair across the room, her legs crossed in a ladylike fashion, symbolizing both modesty and elegance. And she still looked like a seductress. One whose scent was driving him crazy. Cobra wanted her, but in ways he couldn't have her, he'd have to limit himself to kissing her for now. But it was going to be tough.

After taking a few more sips of coffee, instead of sitting on the sofa, he placed the cup back in the saucer and walked over to her. He wasn't there for small talk, and they both knew it.

*****

Desiree watched Cobra set the coffee cup down and begin walking toward her, hearing her breath hitch in her throat with every step he took. Her senses were on full alert, electrified like the rest of her body. It wasn't just the *Cobra Sexy Stroll* that was getting to her. His seductive aroma sent a wave of awareness rushing through her.

Upon reaching her, he closed in, one hand braced on each side of the chair. The intense look in the depths of his dark eyes sent a wave of desire rippling through her. His gaze was fixed on her, holding her captive, while sexual tension and heat built between them. An undeniable magnetism hummed in the air, making it thick with unspoken possibilities.

"Cobra…" She breathed his name.

"I'm here, Desiree."

Yes, he most certainly was, and her desire to be kissed by him was almost overwhelming. He leaned in closer and, with the tip of his tongue, began gently tracing her lips, earlobes, and the side of her neck. This time, his name escaped her lips in a moan, and that was when he captured her mouth in his, and pulled her from the chair and into his arms.

*****

Cobra had thought of kissing her during the play. Each time he glanced at her, as she smiled at a scene on stage, he wished he could whisk her away and kiss that smile from her lips.

Now she was here, in his arms, his lips locked with hers, and he refused to rush. He wanted to savor this moment and the ones that followed. Tonight was all about strategic planning, building her desire, and priming her for what was to come. It would be a different kind of foreplay for him, but it was all the richer because he knew the reward would be worth it.

Because they had kissed several times before, he knew—and loved—what she tasted like. But tonight he wanted them to take things slowly, allowing both of them to savor the flavors they already knew, and lose themselves in the intoxicating blend of their own aromas. He wanted to know more than just what her mouth tasted like; he wanted to taste her skin all over. Every inch of her body. But not all of it tonight.

Without breaking their kiss, he effortlessly swept her into his arms and sat, bringing her down on his lap. Anticipating the way her dress would ride up, he allowed his hand to softly stroke the bare skin of her thighs and loved the sound of her moans as he did.

She abruptly pulled away from the kiss, trapping his gaze with her own, her breath catching in a rapid rhythm that matched his. The look in the depths of her hazel eyes was filled with a desire so raw that his already aroused body got harder. He had no doubt she could feel his erection poking her backside. Would she climb out of his lap and ask him to leave, thinking what they were sharing was way too much for a first date? Or was she curious to see just how far he would go in giving her the kiss he thought she deserved?

Their gazes held, and then she leaned in and pressed her lips to his. He took her mouth again, hungrier than before. The choice to continue had been hers, and he would definitely oblige her...within his limitations. The feel of her skin made staying within his restraints difficult. Touching her enticed him to lift her up, unzip his pants, shift her body so he could enter her, and...

The sudden, blinding temptation made Cobra break the kiss with a gasp. Their gazes locked, their breathing equally uneven. He studied her—lips swollen from his kisses, eyes glazed with passion—and knew there was no way he could end things now. He had to finish what he'd started. Although he would not be fully satisfied with tonight's encounter, he was determined that she would be.

He slightly shifted her in his lap before taking her mouth again. The moment their tongues began tangling, he eased his hand between her legs and pushed aside her panties, finding her womanly core hot and wet. And then he slid his finger inside and began stroking her clit. He massaged both sides of it, deliberately stimulating it with circular motions, determined to identify her erogenous zones.

The mating of their tongues increased, turning the kiss desperate, feverish, and nearly uncontrolled. Her moans became more urgent, as if she wanted a deeper connection. His finger moved inside of her relentlessly, in rhythm with the sounds she was making. In his own way, he was staking his claim on her body, the same way he'd done with her mouth the first time they'd kissed. She began moving on his lap, rocking her hips, and pressing her body upward against his hand.

Desiree suddenly broke off the kiss with a groan and met his gaze. He recognized the look in her eyes, saw what she was fighting against.

"Let it go, Desiree. Come for me, baby."

***

As if her body was reacting to his command, Desiree cried out Cobra's name as an orgasm of gigantic proportions ripped into her. She screamed, digging her fingernails into the arms holding her, while her body pushed harder against his hand. He maintained a meticulous rhythm with his finger, drawing out the experience for her, and deliberately extending the peak of her pleasure.

She could not recall at what point her orgasm ended. However, she thought she'd never forget how he stood with her in his arms and moved toward her bedroom, where he placed her on the bed and joined her there. They were both fully clothed. He held her in his arms while her body gradually returned to normal. At least she assumed that was what was supposed to happen, but wasn't sure if it could. Her heart was still pumping wildly, and the area between her legs remained stimulated.

He held her for a long moment before leaning over to brush a kiss on her lips. Then he was kissing her in a way that was making her moan again. Breaking off the kiss, he whispered that he would check on her tomorrow, and would arm the security system before leaving. Then he released her and eased from the bed. She shifted her position to watch him.

He paused at her bedroom door and looked back at her, met her gaze, and held it. Then he purposely licked his finger—the one he'd had inside her—before giving her a sensuous smile and walking out.

She lay there. Too exhausted to move. Her body had reached a peak of pleasure it had never experienced before, and she felt enraptured. It was as if her entire being was filled with overwhelming emotions. Some she couldn't define or explain.

Before drifting off to sleep, she thought about what she'd overheard from those women that day. They hadn't been wrong about Cobra Masters's skills in the bedroom. If this was him not having sex, she couldn't help wondering how incredible it could be if they did.

Just thinking about that made her smile.

***

Hours later, Cobra climbed into bed, his body thrumming with a sharp, unsatisfied ache that settled deep in his lower extremities. At the same time, he felt a sense of pride settle in his chest. He'd given Desiree a night to remember. And she deserved it. Tonight, bringing her pleasure had meant more to him than experiencing his own. He could wait for that, though, after tonight, it would be even more torturous for him.

He closed his eyes, remembering the sound of Desiree scream his name and seeing her come apart in his arms. And she looked beautiful while doing it. What was even more powerful was the way their gazes had connected at the exact moment an orgasm had coursed through her, right before she had closed her eyes in what seemed like unaltered bliss.

And the kiss they had shared tonight, the one he hadn't wanted to end, had proven just how incredibly hot she was. She had matched his kiss, stroke for stroke. Had claimed his tongue as hers, just as he had claimed hers.

A few weeks ago, she had mentioned a former lover and how sexually incompatible they'd been. He hoped she knew now that that wouldn't be the case with them, that what they shared tonight was a prelude of how things would be with them.

And the thought that he had lain in bed with her in his arms afterwards, fully clothed. That had been a first for him, but he had needed that time with her while her body returned to some semblance of normalcy after being transported beyond the stars. His chest expanded at knowing that he had been the one to take her there.

His phone rang, and Cobra recognized the caller. Grabbing his cell phone off the nightstand, he answered it. "You're calling rather late, aren't you, Landon?"

He heard his friend's chuckle. "I couldn't sleep, so I figured I would bother you."

"What's keeping you up?"

"Alexia, Raejean, and Brandy are in town for Taye's birthday. Monica and all the other female Bennett cousins joined them to celebrate. Whenever Monica goes out without me, I can't sleep until I know she's back home, safe and sound."

Alexia, Raejean, Brandy, and Taye were Monica's older cousins who had acted as mentors to the younger generation of female Bennetts.

Landon continued, "Besides, I wanted to wrap up that report you hired me to get on Allison Desiree Sharpe. Expect to receive it the middle of next week. I will text you with the tracking information."

Cobra had forgotten all about the report. "Sounds good."

"Are you ready for the Masters Family Reunion next weekend? Of course, Monica and I are coming."

"Then I guess I'll be seeing you then."

"Are you bringing anyone?"

Cobra frowned. His brothers had asked him the same question earlier in the week. "I've never brought anyone to the family reunion, and I'm not starting now."

And because he figured Landon knew about the bet, he added, "The last thing I need is for my brothers to think they're going to win our bet."

Now that Colton had returned from his honeymoon, he was making a nuisance of himself by calling every day to check on him. With three months left to go, his brothers were getting nervous about the possibility of losing.

"If you say so. I saw how you were holding on to Allison Sharpe at Colton's wedding."

Cobra rolled his eyes. "Goodnight, Landon. I'll look forward to getting that report next week."

"Okay. I'll text you when to expect it."

After ending the call, Cobra settled into a comfortable position in bed. His family and friends had it all wrong if they assumed something serious was going on between him and Desiree. Granted, he intended to sleep with her, but that was after his period of self-imposed celibacy was over and not before. Now, if he could only convince his libido to hold on until satisfaction day, he would make sure it was well worth the wait.

***

"Kassie, do you realize what you're saying?" Léandre Beauchamp asked his sister. He had placed her call on speaker while he moved around the cabin.

"I know exactly what I'm suggesting, Dre. It's about time you let Camille know how you feel about her."

"I can't do that."

"Why not?"

"I might lose her friendship, and I couldn't handle it if that were to happen."

"You won't lose anything. The two of you have been best friends forever. But anyone with eyes can see that there's more to it. I've seen how the two of you watch each other when you think no one is looking. She has it as bad for you as you have it for her."

He wished like hell that was true. "I doubt that."

"Well, I don't. You've finished the script and still have two and a half weeks left to spend at the cabin. I think you should invite her to join you. You never know. Once you're in close proximity, you might realize there is more between the two of you than friendship."

Léandre rolled his eyes. "There is, and it's all on my side."

"I honestly don't think that's the case, Dre. And don't you owe it to yourself to find out the truth once and for all?"

He released a deep sigh as he looked around. The cabin had plenty of room—three bedrooms, each with its own bath, a huge eat-in kitchen, living room, dining room, and a huge entertainment loft. All the windows had beautiful views of the snow-capped mountains. If he invited her here, he knew Camille would love it. And the place was so big, she could have all the privacy she wanted. If she wanted it...

Kassie had discovered his secret: he was hopelessly in love with Camille. His sister had happened upon a book of poems he had written for Camille but never given to her. When she'd questioned him about it, he'd admitted the truth. And she hadn't left him alone since.

"Fine, I'll do it. But if you're wrong and I lose Camille as a friend, I'll never speak to you again."

Kassie chuckled. "You're my older brother, so you have to talk to me. But don't worry. You won't lose her. And after all these years, I'll finally get to claim her as a real sister. Now, what are you going to say to get her here? It has to sound convincing."

It was time to end this. Otherwise, she'd plan out his whole life for him. "Goodbye, Kassie."

"Goodbye, Big Brother."

After ending the call with his sister, Léandre decided to call Camille...while he still had the nerve to do it.

CHAPTER 11

When Desiree woke up the next morning, she felt more well-rested than she'd ever been. It didn't matter that she had slept in the outfit she had worn on her date last night. Her entire body felt different, as if there were lingering effects, some remaining afterglow from a night like none other. She felt entrenched in a calm born of total physical satisfaction.

And she knew why.

But how in the world had a single orgasm done that? Granted, it was the first she'd had in years —five years, specifically. The night she'd spent with Aimery two years ago didn't count since he hadn't done anything for her.

And the times she'd spent with her boyfriend, Eddie Baylor, in her sophomore year of college in Memphis... Well, there was no comparison. Back then, the sensation had been over in a quick minute. After three tries, she had decided sex was overrated and decided to focus on her studies instead.

Last night, Cobra had proven her wrong, showing her that it wasn't about the sexual act itself, but the man you shared it with. And it had all started with a kiss... Not only had he given her pleasure, but he had proved himself a true master, amplifying the sensations and pushing her to the brink of desire. What man took the time to do that during a kiss? Especially when that kiss was all he would be getting, and all that pleasure he gave her wasn't reciprocated. He had made last night about her and not himself.

As she eased out of bed to take a shower, her phone rang, and recognizing the ringtone, she quickly walked to the living room to pull it out of her purse. "Hi Cam."

"Rae, you won't believe what happened."

Hearing the excitement in Camille's voice, Desiree settled down into the chair that she and Cobra had shared last night. "So, what happened?"

"Léandre called."

Desiree nodded. Since Camille and Léandre had been friends for years and he would often call her, she figured there had to be more. "And...?"

"And he invited me to join him in the Swiss Alps for two weeks."

Desiree smiled. "Alrighty now. Are you going to go?"

"Oh yeah, I'm going. He's paying my way there and will be waiting for me when I arrive at the airport in Switzerland. Then we'll catch the train to the mountains where the cabin he's been using is located."

"When do you leave?"

"Tomorrow."

"Tomorrow? Why so soon? Will you be able to get ready that quickly?"

"My packing cubes are already organized. All I have to do is arrange them in my luggage. However, I did have to switch out summer clothes for outfits that will keep me warm. And Melia agreed to water the plants in the apartment while I'm gone. It's only for two weeks."

"Sounds like fun."

"He said he's inviting me because he wants me to read the script he just finished, that he values my opinion."

"Hmm, there's no reason for you to go all the way to the Swiss Alps just to do that. He could have emailed it. I think he just wants you there with him."

"You really think so?"

Desiree heard the hopefulness in her voice. "Don't you?"

"I'm too afraid to think that, Rae. So, I'm getting on that plane tomorrow with no expectations. I don't want to be disappointed."

"And if the opportunity arises where you could make your feelings for him known, will you take it?" Desiree asked.

Camille didn't say anything for a minute and then quickly said, "Yes, I will take it. It's about time, don't you think?"

"It's not about what I think, Cam. It's about what you think."

Camille was silent for a few more moments. Obviously, she was terrified to take this next step. "Then yes, I think it's about time."

Desiree chuckled. "I think so, too."

"So, how was your date last night?" Camille asked.

Desiree smiled and looked down at her dress—the same dress Cobra's hands had slipped underneath last night. "Cam, you won't believe what happened."

"Tell me everything, Rae," she said, laughing.

She couldn't do that—not all of it. Because she couldn't help wanting to keep a part of last night's magic all to herself.

***

Cobra placed his tennis racket in the closet and glanced around his home. He had moved to Harlem at the beginning of the year, after living in Manhattan for nearly eight years. He had felt it was time to move out of the condo and had purchased the four-story brownstone. He loved living here; the community was great, and everything he needed was an easy commute.

But today was the first time he'd looked around his home and thought it felt lonely. When he lived in Manhattan, he'd been known to throw a party or two at his condo, especially when bringing in the New Year. And he was the one who threw yearly birthday celebrations for himself and his brothers.

As well, the condo was the place he'd invite women to spend time with him—women whose names he couldn't now remember. He hadn't thought twice about taking his date to his place instead of suggesting they go to a hotel. That open-door policy ended after his evening with Bernice Whey. Hell, he'd even given the bedroom furniture from his Savannah home to one of his younger cousins. Just remembering the night Allison/Bernice had spread out on his bed made him feel ill.

When he moved into the six-bedroom, four-bath brownstone, he decided it was time to purchase all new furniture. And he promised himself that the place would be all his. No more hookups in his personal space. But then, after hearing about the way Bernice had tricked her baby daddies at hotels, he wasn't sure they were the safest places for one-night stands, either.

Needing a shower, he headed for the bedroom, pulling his phone out of his back pocket as he walked. He'd woken up that morning thinking about Desiree, but hadn't wanted to call her too soon, since she'd said she would be sleeping late. He checked his watch. It was after noon—she should be up by now.

He'd hated leaving her to sleep in the dress she had worn on their date, but the only alternative was to undress her and put her in something else. He knew the limits to his willpower and control where she was concerned, and undressing her would have been pushing it too far. So he chose the safer option and left.

"Hello?"

Why did the sound of her voice cause him to pause? And why had his heart seemed to skip a beat? Drawing in a deep breath, he responded, "Good afternoon. I'm just checking in to see how you're doing."

"I'm good. I owe you big time for the best sleep ever. Thank you."

He moved the phone from his ear and stared at it before returning it to his ear again. He hadn't expected to hear that admission from her. What a change in attitude. Was one kiss —and a bit more —responsible for it? In that case, he'd give her plenty more like it. All guaranteed to turn up the heat.

He smiled, deciding not to pretend he had no idea what she was referring to. "Anytime," he said, walking into his bathroom.

"I'd advise you to tread carefully with that offer, Cobra Masters. I might take you up on it."

He took a steady breath. Was she flirting with him? "I've been duly warned. What are your plans for the week?"

"Hmm, I really enjoyed ice skating the other night, and might do it again this week. And there's a show at the Apollo on Tuesday night that I plan to check out."

"By yourself?"

The sound of her chuckle had heat simmering inside of him. "Yes, by myself. I'm a big girl."

He didn't know about her being a big girl, but she was definitely a perfect woman. "Well, enjoy the rest of your day, Desiree, as well as your week."

"You, too, Cobra, and if I don't talk to you before you leave for Savannah, enjoy your family reunion."

"Thanks."

He ended the call, placed the phone on the bathroom vanity, and leaned against it. When had a phone conversation with a woman stirred such deep, burning desire in him? If an evening of sensual fun had made her this compliant, he couldn't wait until they finally shared a bed. He was counting down the next three months now more so than ever.

He wasn't flying out to Savannah until Thursday morning, and he wanted to see her again before he left town. Although he knew security was good at her condo, he didn't like the thought of her being at the ice rink alone. Nor did the thought of her going to the Apollo by herself sit well with him.

He shook his head. Why was he acting like this? Being protective of a woman felt new to him, since there were few females in the Masters family—at least in his generation. Quinece was older and had always been capable of taking care of herself. Besides, she was a twin to his cousin Quinn, and from what he'd heard, Quinece had been the fighter, and Quinn, the negotiator. That made sense since Quinn was now a high-powered entertainment attorney.

Deciding not to worry about it, he thought of the week ahead. He liked the idea of seeing her again before he left town on Thursday. That was three days from now...and he intended to spend all three with her.

With that decision made, he began undressing for his shower.

***

Sydney, Australia

"What are you thinking about, Richard?"

Richard Sharpe smiled at the feel of the warm, feminine arms that wrapped around him from behind. He was standing at the hotel's window, looking out at the Sydney Harbour Bridge.

It was hard to believe he had found love again at his age. Lolita was everything he needed in his life, and he was glad to have met her when he had. In addition to being a very beautiful woman, she had a heart of gold.

"I'm wondering what your daughter and son-in-law think about you staying at the hotel with me while I'm in town."

He would spend time in Sydney with Lolita, her daughter, and her family —at least for a week. Then he and Lolita would spend some time in Brisbane before flying to New Zealand. They would return to Sydney a few days before he returned to the States. It had been years since he had taken a real vacation, and he wanted to spend all his time with her.

She moved to face him and stood, her arms still around him, then smiled. It was that same smile that had captured his heart the day they had met. "After meeting you, I'm sure they think I am one lucky woman," she said. "They know I am old enough to make my own decisions about what I want to do and who I want to be with. And I give my children the same respect."

She paused before saying. "Both of my kids—my son and my daughter—were really worried about me after their father died, and for the past six years, I've assured them that I was okay. But it wasn't until I met you that I realized how it feels to live again."

It had taken nearly twice that long for him to figure out the same thing. "I just want you to be sure about everything, sweetheart," he said.

"I am. This is where I want to be. You've gotten to know Keith—who can be rather protective of me, to put it mildly—and he likes you a lot. Vivian does, too. She told me so after dinner. My kids chose their spouses well, though I have to admit I was worried when Vivian decided to move to Harrison's home in Sydney after they married. But she is so happy, and now with the baby to keep her busy, she is even happier."

Richard nodded. "And I'd like to go on record to say I like them, too. You have a beautiful family."

"Thank you."

"Now," Lolita said, pulling him toward the sofa in the suite, "come tell me how things are going with your granddaughter."

He sat and pulled Lolita into his lap. They both liked their cuddle time. "I'm glad she's home," he said, tightening his arms around her. "As I've said before, I might have made mistakes in the past regarding Allison, but I want to correct them, Lolita. I want to get to know my granddaughter."

"And you should. All kids go through growing pains. I told you about the trouble I had with Vivian after Doug died. She went a little wild and refused to do anything productive with her life. When she finally settled down, she enrolled at NYU, and then met Harrison. It was only afterwards that I discovered her rebellion was the only way she knew to fight the grief she felt over losing Doug. She'd been a daddy's girl. From what you told me, Richard, it sounded like Allison had a rough time of it early on, and I'm sure she's experiencing some deep feelings. You need to find out just what's going on with her. The two of you need to have what they call a good 'come to Jesus moment'.

"We will. And I will tell her about you and maybe set something up for the two of you to meet when you return to the States after Labor Day."

"I'm looking forward to that. How is she doing at the Sharpe Corporation?"

"Very well. My executive team is impressed with her. She seems to enjoy being there and came ready to roll up her sleeves and learn all she can."

"You know what I think, Richard?"

"I think you're about to tell me, sweetheart." He grinned.

"You know me well," she said, chuckling. "I have a feeling that Allison was ready to come home and was just waiting for your call."

"She could have come home at any time," he said.

Lolita shrugged. "Maybe she felt that she couldn't."

He nodded, thinking about that. "I truly want a relationship with my granddaughter to work."

"Then work on it."

He nodded. "Something is going on between her and Cobra."

"Something like what?"

"Not sure. They claim they dislike each other."

Lolita smiled. "They might, but I discovered when Keith and April first met, that love and hate are two sides of the same coin. They disliked each other intensely! And though they still don't agree on everything, they love each other immensely and are perfect for each other. I couldn't have hoped for a better wife for Keith."

"Well, I'm not sure what's going on between Cobra and Allison. But whatever it is, I intend to stay out of it and let them work it out."

"That's a good idea. Now, do you know what else is a good idea?"

"No, what?"

"For you were to take me into the bedroom and show me how much you've missed me."

Richard stood with her in his arms. "That would be my absolute pleasure, sweetheart."

CHAPTER 12

When the intercom sounded on her desk, Desiree glanced up from the documents she was reading. "Yes, Karlie?"

"Ms. Sharpe, there's someone here to see you."

Desiree raised a brow. "Who?"

"A man."

Desiree shook her head and was about to ask if the man had a name, but figured there was only one man who could make her very efficient administrative assistant sound so breathy. He was the same man who had shown up unexpectedly at the condo's ice skating rink on Monday night. She had just finished her warmups, and when she had felt a presence, she had looked up to see him standing there, leaning against the wall with his hands shoved in his pockets, watching her intently.

Then, without saying anything, he walked over and sat on the bench, obviously planning to watch her skate. For some reason, having him there didn't bother her. Instead, it had filled her with an inner peace that she hadn't known in a while. And she'd skated well that night. Her jumps and spins had been fluid, and she could feel the music in her movements. And when she had taken her bow for the night, he had stood and clapped. Then he'd walked her back to her condo, kissed her at her door, made sure she got inside, and had left.

Last night, he had again shown up unexpectedly, cancelling her ride with Ron, to take her to the Apollo. Not only had he driven her there, but he also stayed by her side. They'd enjoyed the show, then stopped at a café for dessert and coffee after. When he brought her home, he kissed her goodnight and left her limp with desire...again.

Cobra hadn't said anything about seeing her today, but it would be just like him to show up without calling first. He'd already done it twice this week. But she wasn't complaining. In fact, she'd been kind of hoping to see him again before he left town.

"Please send Mr. Masters in. Oh, and Karlie, feel free to take your lunch now." The last thing she wanted was for her assistant to wonder what was or was not going on in her office.

"Mr. Masters? His name is not Mr. Masters," Karlie whispered.

Desiree raised a brow, confused. "Then who is it?"

"Mr. LeBlanc. Aimery LeBlanc. The French race car driver that's always in the news," Karlie whispered even lower.

Desiree frowned. What in the world was Aimery doing here? She hadn't heard from him in more than two years. The night their affair had ended hadn't been pretty. "Please send Mr. LeBlanc in, Karlie."

She got up from her desk and moments later, Aimery walked in, smiling.

Smiling? He was a good-looking man, she would have to give him that much. And there was no telling how much he had paid for that designer suit. But that was all he had—good looks and no substance. As Camille would say, he was all show and no go. All icing with no cake.

She smiled back, deciding she could act just as fake as he was. "Aimery, what a surprise." She refused to go so far as to say it was a pleasant surprise, because it wasn't. "What are you doing here?"

She offered him a chair when it looked as if he was coming toward her desk. To do what? Certainly not to offer her a peck on the cheek. She didn't even want a courtesy kiss on the hand from him. They hadn't ended things with a lasting friendship in mind. When he slid into the chair, she realized that truly, there was nothing sexy about the way he moved. At least, not compared to Cobra.

Even though she knew it wasn't fair, she couldn't help comparing the two men. And Aimery was lacking in so many ways. Although both he and Cobra were handsome men and sharp dressers, that was where the similarities ended. She no longer found him attractive in the least, and whatever sexual chemistry they had before was long gone. Whereas the chemistry between her and Cobra was off the charts.

However, she already knew the main difference between the men lay in how they conducted themselves in the bedroom. Aimery was a selfish bastard, and though she hadn't slept with Cobra yet, she already knew it would be something she'd never forget.

When she took her seat behind her desk, she tightened her thighs together when she remembered the way Cobra had so easily brought her to a climax. She'd been thinking of that a lot lately, almost every single day. The memory often made her feel hot and needy, and lately, she'd been thinking of ways to return the favor. She couldn't help thinking Cobra would likely approve of some of the ideas she had come up with.

"I'm in America doing several late-night talk shows to promote my next big race. But that's not the reason I'm here, right now. This weekend, I discovered in conversing with someone that you'd kept something from me when we were together, *ma chérie,*" Aimery said, intruding into her salacious thoughts.

She was about to tell him he could take his words of endearment and shove them somewhere, but resisted. She wasn't his anything—definitely not his darling or sweetheart.

Still, she was curious about his motives for being here. Why would her name have come up in any of his conversations, and just what did he think she had kept from him? "What is it that you think I didn't tell you, Aimery?" she asked, leaning back in her chair.

"That you were Richard Sharpe's granddaughter. I had the honor of dining in the home of Geoff Timberlake Saturday night, and I noticed a group of pictures sitting on one of the tables. He'd taken them at a wedding of a business associate last month. One of those photos was of Geoff standing beside a man he pointed out as a close friend. Of course, I recognized him as Richard Sharpe. Then I recognized you standing beside him. I assumed you were his trophy date, but Geoff informed me that you were his granddaughter who had recently moved back home from Paris."

She nodded. Geoff Timberlake was an old friend of her grandfather's, and she recalled when the photo had been taken at Colton's wedding.

"And?" she asked, since he had yet to say why it was any of his business.

"And imagine my surprise. Your relationship to Richard Sharpe would have been good to know about when we were a couple."

She lifted a brow. *Seriously*? "And it would have benefited you how?" she asked.

He chuckled. "You want a list? At the top, Richard Sharpe could have become one of my major sponsors on the circuit. Hell, I would have even overlooked your, ahh...sexual inadequacies had I known."

Her sexual inadequacies? She couldn't believe what she was hearing. She was about to tell him what he could do with his inadequate body part when a deep, male voice said, "You must have Desiree mixed up with someone else. I know for a fact there's not an inadequate bone in her body. Sexual or otherwise."

Desiree glanced beyond Aimery and saw Cobra standing in the doorway. Did he not believe in knocking? Still, she was glad to see him. Judging from the look on his face, he was furious, and like the snake he was named for, he seemed poised to strike. Dangerous but sexy. A thrill ran through her as she stood. "Cobra?"

"Desiree," he said, coming into her office and closing the door behind him. Crossing the room, he brushed a kiss across her lips, deliberately exposing the degree of familiarity between them.

Even the chaste kiss was swoon-worthy. When she recovered her composure, she went to introduce the two men. "Cobra, this is Aimery, and —"

"And he was just leaving," Cobra boldly interrupted.

She glanced at Cobra, saw the intense rage in the depths of his eyes, and could even feel anger seeping out of him—anger on her behalf. She couldn't help feeling a quiet satisfaction that he'd defended her against Aimery's comment. Unlike her ex, Cobra was all show and a lot of go. He wouldn't hesitate to prove it by knocking the hell out of Aimery. Hadn't her grand-father once told her that Cobra was a man who could hold his own?

Deciding to avoid any type of confrontation between the two men, she said, "Yes, Aimery was leaving."

Aimery's stare moved angrily from Desiree to Cobra, and then back to Desiree again. "I came to take you to lunch, Desiree, for old times' sake."

"Yeah, that won't be happening," Cobra said stiffly.

Anger spread across Aimery's features. He stood glaring at them both, but his next words were directed at her. "I'm staying at the Ritz-Carlton, room 3410. I will be in New York through the weekend. When you start speaking for yourself again, Desiree, you can find me there. Don't wait too long." Then he walked out of her office and slammed the door behind him.

"Asshole," Cobra and Desiree said simultaneously, then looked at each other and grinned.

"I should have kicked his ass," Cobra said.

"What you should have done was knock, or at least let Karlie announce you."

"Who's Karlie?"

"She's my administrative assistant."

He shrugged. "She must have gone to lunch because no one was sitting at the desk out front."

Desiree had forgotten that she'd suggested that Karlie go to lunch when she thought her visitor had been him. "Yes, she must have gone to lunch. Why are you here, Cobra?"

"To take you to lunch."

"You don't believe in calling first, the same way you don't believe in knocking?"

He smiled. "What I believe in, Ms. Sharpe, is keeping you surprised and on your toes. I like making that sharp mind of yours even sharper. Now grab your purse and let's go."

She was about to tell him that she did not like being bossed around when he pulled her into his arms and kissed her. She hadn't expected the kiss, but she sure did welcome it. He slid his tongue deep inside her mouth, then began having his way with hers. She couldn't fight back the moan his kiss elicited. It was as if she couldn't get enough of him.

They were interrupted by the buzz of the intercom on her desk. Breaking the kiss, she licked her lips before reaching behind her and pressing the button. Desiree drew in a deep breath, released it, and then, in the most composed voice she could muster, said, "Yes, Karlie?"

She must have still sounded rather breathy since Karlie hesitated a moment before answering, "I just wanted to let you know I'm back from lunch, Ms. Sharpe."

Desiree drew in another deep breath and released it. "Okay. Thanks for letting me know."

She looked at Cobra, and before she could say anything, he leaned in, lightly chafing his beard across her jaw before kissing her again. This kiss was brief but just as potent. Then he looked her up and down and said, "You look very nice today."

"Thanks." She was wearing a red pantsuit. Conservative enough for the office but still flattering. She received numerous compliments today, even one from Saul Lawrence, her grandfather's second-in-command.

"Come on, let's get out of here before we get into trouble," Cobra said.

She nodded, then opened one of the drawers to her desk and grabbed her purse. He took her hand, and when they walked out of her office, she saw the surprise on Karlie's face. She almost laughed. When Karlie had gone for lunch, Desiree had one handsome man in her office. Now she was walking out with another one.

But this one was far superior, in Desiree's opinion. Cobra had more masculinity in his pinkie finger than Aimery had in his entire body. "I'm leaving for lunch now, Karlie."

Her administrative assistant's eyes were glued to Cobra, as if spellbound, when she answered, "Alright, Ms. Sharpe."

Desiree inwardly smiled, understanding Karlie's reaction completely.

***

By the time they walked into the Whirlwind Restaurant, some of the anger had left Cobra's body. Some of it, but not all. He knew the hotel where the man was staying. Hell, thanks to the guy's big mouth, he even knew his room number. What he should do is pay the bastard a surprise visit and beat the hell out of him for what he had said to Desiree.

He hoped she hadn't believed what Aimery LeBlanc had said about her sexual inadequacies. But she'd mentioned it once before, so he knew it bothered her, at least a little.

Cobra was looking forward to proving to Desiree just how wrong that sorry excuse for a man was. Now more than ever, he was glad that he had given her the kind of kiss she had deserved last Saturday night. He knew it had likely been Aimery who'd dropped the ball in the bedroom and placed the blame on her. What an ass.

He doubted Desiree had any idea how hard it had been to kiss her goodnight at her door the last two nights and leave.

He had been so tempted to go inside with her and offer her a repeat of Saturday night. Only, instead of his finger, he would have used his tongue.

"Do you want a private room, Mr. Masters?" the maître d' asked.

"Yes. The Belgium will work, Thomas, if it's not being used." The Belgium Room was where he frequently met with his clients for lunch to discuss sensitive matters and ensure maximum discretion.

"It's not reserved. This way, please." The man led them to the back of the spacious restaurant and toward a bank of elevators.

"Why do we need a private room?" Desiree leaned in to ask.

"So that we can talk privately."

She frowned at him. "If you plan to ask me anything about Aimery, forget it. Nothing about him is open for discussion. What we shared ended over two years ago."

As far as Cobra was concerned, she hadn't shared anything with the man. At least nothing solid. "Whatever." She would discover soon enough that lovers could talk in other ways.

When he'd awakened that morning, it hit him that he would be leaving town and wouldn't see her for a few days. That bothered him. And after seeing that Aimery guy and knowing the man would be in New York while Cobra was in Savannah, didn't sit well with him, either. What the hell was wrong with him? He was acting like a jealous boyfriend, but the idea was ridiculous. He'd never worried about what a woman was doing before, so why was he doing it now?

"Here you are, Sir," Thomas said, opening the door to the private room. "The menus are on the table. I'll return in a few minutes to take your orders."

"No rush, Thomas. I'll text you when we're ready."

"Yes, Mr. Masters." Then the man left.

Cobra watched Desiree glance around the room with a curious eye. In addition to the dining table, there were a couple of sofas in the room, a private bar, a huge television on the wall, and specialized audiovisual equipment.

The Belgium Room was not only located in the back of the restaurant but also on another floor. Diners had to take an elevator to reach it. The expansive room provided a secluded, intimate atmosphere ideal for discreet, upscale lunches or dinner business meetings. A few years ago, he and four other businessmen formed a co-op to sub-lease this room. Given their clientele, they saw it as a valuable investment. So far, Cobra had always used it for business, but not today.

He removed his jacket and hung it up on a nearby coat rack by the door. Without Desiree noticing, he locked the door, then moved toward her. She certainly looked good today. That red pantsuit looked sexy as hell on her, and the color seemed to make her eyes appear more vibrant. The tunic portion of the pantsuit had a square neckline with a button-down front, and the hem ended just short of her hipline, framing her feminine curves. She looked both professional and sexy.

Desiree took a step back when he approached, assuming he was about to pull out the chair for her to sit at the dining table, then gasped when, instead, he swept her into his arms and carried her over to one of the sofas.

"What do you think you're doing?" she asked in an indignant tone when he sat down with her in his lap.

"I told you we would talk, but there's more than one way to communicate, Desiree. Today I plan to demonstrate another way." Then he swooped down and took her mouth in a sizzling kiss.

CHAPTER 13

When Desiree parted her lips, Cobra's tongue immediately sought entrance, mating with hers with an intensity that melted away any resistance. How could she deny herself this? How often was a woman kissed by a man who so evidently knew what he was doing?

She wasn't sure how long the kiss lasted before they were forced to pull back for air. He stared down at her, and the moment their gazes locked, something passed between them. She wasn't sure what, but knew from the look in his eyes that he had felt it, too. He then lowered his head, and with gentle precision, he traced her mouth with the tip of his tongue, moving from one side to the other.

When she released a moan, Cobra added sensuous nibbling around her mouth into the mix. He began licking downward toward her neck, and her nerve endings went on high alert as he traced kisses all over her collarbone.

Finally, he returned to her mouth to kiss her again. She had been so caught up in the kiss that she hadn't realized he had unbuttoned the top of her pantsuit until she felt a cool blast from the air conditioner hit her chest. She broke off the kiss to stare up at him and saw how dark his pupils had become. He was so aroused that she could feel his erection poking hard against her backside.

"I want to taste your breasts, Desiree. May I?"

She was surprised he had asked. Neither Eddie nor Aimery had. It was as if they'd assumed her breasts had been theirs for the taking. "What if someone were to come in?" she asked, glancing at the door.

"I locked it."

"Oh." Had he brought her here with the intention of seducing her? If so, how far would he take things? Was he willing to forgo his vow of celibacy?

As if he was privy to her thoughts, he said, "I won't go any farther than tasting your breasts, Desiree. No matter how hot things get. I promise."

"You have that much control?" she asked.

He smiled. "I am a very disciplined man."

He was also a man who wasn't telling her everything. Maybe it was time for her to tell him what she knew. But then, as Camille had said, his vow of celibacy was private to him, like her vow was to her. Still, she would be the one who derived pleasure from what he wanted to do, not him. So why was he torturing himself this way?

What man was that noble? None she'd ever come across. He had to be thinking that he would get something out of it eventually. Was it his plan to deliberately keep her all hot and bothered for three more months?

She couldn't see that working out, considering how hot they were for each other now. Her period of celibacy didn't end until January, but she had no qualms about ending it sooner, for him, knowing the depth of pleasure she would receive. Cobra had already proven that he was a giver, not a taker.

All rational thoughts fled her mind when she felt his finger trace along the edge of her red lace bra.

"May I?" he asked, making her realize he was waiting for her permission to proceed. The tip of his finger slowly began circling her nipples through her bra, and the lace material was no match for the feel of him. Nor were the desires building inside of her.

"Yes, you may," she whispered on a moan.

He quickly unsnapped the front clasp of her bra, and she saw the heat that appeared in his eyes when he stared at her bare breasts. "They are beautiful, Desiree."

That was something else neither Eddie nor Aimery had ever done—told her she was beautiful. "Thank you." And she meant it, more than she could ever say.

***

Cobra licked his lips, then lowered his head to take a swollen nipple into his mouth and began sucking on it. He heard Desiree's moan when he increased the pressure.

She had beautiful breasts. They were full and lush, the perfect size and shape. When he had first seen her breasts covered in red lace, straining against the material of her bra, her nipples clearly erect, his arousal had surged. But the moment he had seen them bare, an urgent need had gripped him, and it had taken every ounce of discipline he'd told her he had to hold himself in check.

After removing her bra and top and placing both aside, he cupped the breast in his hand and dipped his head to lick around the darkened nipple, doing swirling motions to it with his tongue before sucking the erect bud into his mouth. At the same time, his other hand lightly caressed the soft skin of the other breast. He could tell she was enjoying herself by the way she arched her back, as if she was trying to shove the nipple deeper into his mouth. He might not be getting any physical pleasure out of this, but his pleasure was knowing that she was and that he was the one giving it to her.

Cobra shifted his attention to the other breast, giving it the same time and affection. He knew the moment she was about to climax. Calling out his name, she reached up to grab hold of his shoulders, then began rocking her hips, as if seeking out what he couldn't give her. He decided to accommodate her in another way, by pressing the palm of his hand in the area between her legs. She felt hot against the material of her pants

He quickly covered her mouth with his to silence her scream that erupted the moment he touched her there, but that didn't stop her body from jerking profusely in his arms.

As it had on Saturday night, her orgasm seemed to go on and on. He didn't mind—he wanted to give her as much pleasure as she could take. When she quieted, he broke off the kiss and looked down at her. She looked beautiful with her eyes closed, flushed face, and swollen lips.

She slowly opened her eyes, looked at him, and asked in a soft voice, "Why do you give me pleasure but not take any for yourself?"

He had known that question would come sooner or later. At least from her. Some women would not have given a damn. They were just as bad as some men. He reached down and gently stroked the side of her face. "Because you deserve it."

"And you don't?"

"Not yet. I want you to get to know me, Desiree."

At that moment, he realized what he had just said was true. He wanted her to know him the way he was starting to know himself. Spending time with her was making him question everything he'd ever thought he wanted in a relationship with a woman. Suddenly, the revolving door to his bedroom seemed cheap, and well, wrong. Did he honestly want to return to that type of lifestyle?

From the very beginning, Desiree had been special. She was nothing like the other women he'd been with. His vow of celibacy had forced him to see, and to accept, that she was different—not a one-and-done type of woman. Nor was she the type that he could toss aside when he'd had his fill. She was one of those women a man looked for in a wife, one he'd love, respect, and honor. The kind he would take home to Mom.

He quickly pushed that notion out of his mind. He was getting ahead of himself. Instead, he told her the truth. "When the time is right, we will come together sexually, Desiree, and share pleasure as you've never felt before. I promise you."

"I believe you, Cobra."

He smiled. Her faith in his abilities touched him, and he lowered his head to kiss her again. This time, it was a gentle kiss, intentionally so. And as his lips touched hers, his mind—and his heart—filled with surprising emotions. What was there between them? And what did he want from her? Although he would miss seeing her over the next few days, he needed that time with his family and friends to put things into perspective.

"Your assistant is going to be wondering where you are. This is a longer lunch than you usually take, I'll bet." He stood with her in his arms and placed her on her feet.

"I'm not worried. I don't have any meetings scheduled for this afternoon."

He reached for her bra and top and helped her put them back on. That was another first. He had undressed a lot of women, but never once had he helped one put her clothes back on. "There's a private bath down that hall if you would like to freshen up."

"Okay. Thanks."

He watched her walk away, admiring that red pantsuit and matching red pumps, while her hair flowed around her shoulders. He knew she'd been wearing a red bra and suspected she was wearing matching panties. Today, she was definitely the lady in red.

When unexpected emotions tugged at him, he concluded that he definitely needed this weekend away from her to think. There had to be a reason why, in such a short period of time, he had allowed Allison Desiree Sharpe to come to mean something to him.

***

Swiss Alps

"So, what do you think of it so far, Camille?"

Camille glanced up and smiled. "I think it's wonderful, Dre. This might be your best play yet."

She saw the smile that formed on his lips and knew her words had pleased him. She had been honest about his work, and of all people, she should know. He had written close to twenty-five plays in his lifetime, five of those when they'd been in high school, and she had acted in every single one of them.

"You're not just saying that, are you?" he asked, coming into the room to sit across from her. She tried not to stare at him. It seemed that the older he got, the more handsome he became. He looked nothing at all like the tall, skinny fifteen-year-old she'd met that first day of school. Now he was built like an athlete and turned feminine heads wherever he went. However, to her, he would always be the boy next door. The one who had captured her heart.

She had arrived in Zurich, Switzerland, three days ago, and he had been at baggage claim, waiting for her. Like the old friends they were, they hugged upon seeing each other, and after grabbing her luggage, they caught a taxi to the train station. The scenic train ride to the Alps had been so beautiful, she had trouble believing her eyes.

"No, I'm not just saying that, Dre. You know me. I can be brutally honest about your work when I need to be. This screenplay is *really* good. Honestly, it's superb. There's just one problem. With all the props you'll need, your budget for this will have to be pretty high."

"I've thought of that."

He leaned closer, and his robust, masculine scent enveloped her, making it difficult to concentrate.

"I haven't told anyone yet, Cam, not even Kassie or my brothers, but I met with Luther Mondruleo a few months ago."

Camille blinked. "*The* Luther Mondruleo?"

Léandre grinned, and Camille's heart skipped a beat. That sexy Léandre grin would be the death of her yet.

"Yes, that's the one. He's one of the wealthiest men in Paris, and his favorite pastime is investing in the arts. After attending one of my productions last year, he did some research on my work, and said he liked what he saw. He asked if I had something new. I told him I didn't, but that I was starting work on something once the play wrapped up. I gave him an overview of my idea, and he loved it. He even offered me the use of this cabin so I could get the first draft written, without any interruptions."

She glanced around. "This is his cabin?"

He nodded. "Sorry about the little white lie. I told Kassie that a friend was letting me use it, because if I told her the truth, she wouldn't leave me alone. You know how my sister is."

She shrugged. "I wasn't too concerned. I just figured you had to have wealthy friends that I don't know."

"You know all my friends, Cam. Even my ex-girlfriends. None of them has this kind of money."

But your family does, she wanted to say. But she didn't. That was a touchy subject with him and had been for years. His parents had four sons, and Léandre was the youngest. The older three had gone to work for the family's corporation after finishing college. However, Léandre's dream had always been to write, produce, and direct plays for a live theater. Paulo Beauchamp had given Dre an ultimatum: either work for the family business or be on his own. Dre had chosen to follow his dream, and to this day hadn't asked his father for anything. Definitely not financial assistance for his plays. Even though he was close to his brothers—and they had offered to invest in his projects—he'd refused to get them involved by accepting any funding behind their father's back.

"Well, I think this script is a winner. And with the right cast, it could be something that could change your life. I'm so happy for you, Dre."

"And I'm happy that you're here with me, Cam. You've always been my biggest supporter."

She grinned. "After twenty-five plays, I would hope so."

"You and I make a great team," he said, standing and crossing the floor to place a kiss on her forehead. That was something he'd started in college. More than once, Desiree had tried to convince her that Dre's forehead kisses meant more than a kiss on the lips.

"How much longer do you think you'll need to finish reading it?" he asked.

She tilted her head to look up at him. "Rushing me back to Paris already?"

"Heck no. I'm just looking forward to our time here together. There's a lot of fun stuff to do—skiing, snowboarding, night sledding, and a lot of other cool stuff. We haven't had that kind of fun in years. So, let's enjoy being here. Just the two of us."

Just the two of us... "I'd like that, Dre."

"Me too."

Was she misreading the moment, or was he looking at her differently? And was her body the only one that was tingling with awareness? When the room got silent, she cleared her throat and said, "I almost forgot. Kassie sent a package for me to give to you."

"Oh? What is it?"

"I don't know. It's in a box. I finished unpacking today and saw it. Hold on, I'll go get it since it might be important." Sliding by him, she rushed off.

***

Léandre watched her leave and let out a deep breath. He couldn't mess this up. He couldn't and wouldn't. Over the next couple of weeks, they would spend time together and get to know each other again.

In a way that sounded weird, since it often seemed as if they had known each other forever. She'd always been his biggest supporter, not just by keeping him motivated but also by playing a role in every one of his theatrical projects, even when they were in college. Although she had continued on to graduate school and then her PhD, she still had his back by helping out where she could, working on sets, and acting as an extra. Last year, when his lead actress got mad and quit in the middle of production, Camille had learned the lines quickly, then took the actress's place.

She had become an overnight sensation and had received excellent reviews. And she had remained the lead throughout the whole production, even though she was doing clinicals for her psychology residency during the day.

Camille was the best buddy a guy could have, but he wanted more. He had always wanted more, but he'd been too afraid to take the first step. Now that she was here, he would do everything he could to convince her that they belonged together. Just before she'd left the room, he'd felt something new, something strong flowing between them. Sexual chemistry. Had she felt it, too?

"Here you are," she said, returning with a wrapped box and handing it to him. Their hands touched in the process, and she drew in a sharp breath the same moment that he did.

"Thanks. I wonder what she sent."

"I don't know. It looks like she wanted it to be a surprise."

He smiled and headed for his bedroom. Closing the door, he began unwrapping the package. There was a note attached that read... *"Dre, I thought it was time you gave this to the person it was intended for."*

He opened the box...and found his book of poems.

CHAPTER 14

Cobra would have to admit that his brother looked happy, and he knew it was all because of the woman by his side. The woman he had married a few months ago. "If Colton ever gives you trouble, Kelly, just know you can ditch him and that I'm available."

Kelly threw her head back and laughed. "I'll keep that in mind."

"You better not," Colton said, pulling his wife closer to his side. "There are some things we never shared, and we won't start now. She is completely taken," he said, leaning in to place a kiss on her wife's lips.

Cobra would admit he was happy for Colton and Cortez. He couldn't help wondering if he would be so lucky one day. He then frowned at the thought that he would wonder about such a thing. Hell, he wasn't sure any woman could hold his interest for long.

At that moment, thoughts of Desiree flashed through his mind. His desire girl. He couldn't help but recall the hot kisses they had shared a few days ago in the Belgium Room.

"Any reason you have a silly-looking grin on your face, Cobra?"

For a minute, he had forgotten his brother and sister-in-law were still there. "I don't have any silly-looking grin on my face."

"You do, too." Colton then turned to Kelly. "Doesn't he?"

She shook her head, grinning. "I refuse to let you pull me into that."

Cobra winked at her. "You're not only gorgeous, but you're smart as a whip, Kelly."

When some of their other cousins approached, the subject changed to other things, such as any plans being made for a Masters' Christmas get-together. It was only a short while later that Cobra decided to go outside to sit in the civic center's courtyard, where the family reunion was being held. Today had been a busy day, and he was glad that in an hour or so, another family reunion would be coming to an end.

***

"The family reunion turned out great, Cobra. You and your committee did an awesome job on it."

Cobra glanced over at Quinn, one of his older cousins who owned a massive law firm in Los Angeles. He was also married to Grammy-award-winning artist Alexia Bennett Masters. Cobra and his brothers were blessed with older cousins they could look up to as they grew up. Quinn and his brothers—Grey, Lake, and Shane—had always been there to offer an ear and advice when needed. Now that the triplets were adults, he especially appreciated that the 'Brothers Four', as they were often called, never pried but were always ready to listen.

"Thanks, but it wasn't all up to me. Aunt Gertrude drafted my services."

Quinn chuckled. "She's done that to all of us at some point or another. It was your turn."

"Whatever." Cobra took a sip of his beer and looked around. "Hayes seemed to enjoy himself."

"He told me that he did," Quinn said, sliding into the chair across from Cobra in the courtyard. "Of course, he's still getting to know everyone. The past year hasn't been easy for him. To lose both parents the way he did, and then to have to leave his friends behind and start over in a new state, a new school, and a family he'd never met. But he's managing. He's doing well in school, and he told me that he signed up for the softball team."

"That's great! It's hard to believe it was a year ago when you got that call."

Social Services in Philadelphia had contacted Quinn to let him know that Sonny, his grandfather Kenneth's grandson, whom he hadn't known about, and his wife had been killed in a robbery. They'd told Quinn that unless a family member applied for custody of Hayes, Sonny's child, the boy would be placed in the foster care system. When they sent Quinn a picture of Hayes, Quinn could tell the boy was a Masters. He favored most of them.

The 'Brothers Four' immediately flew to Philly to claim Hayes. Quinn had claimed full custody since Hayes was the same age as Quinn and Alexia's daughter, Idella. They were in the same grade and could attend the same school.

Quinn got up and grabbed a beer from the cooler, and when he sat back down, Cobra asked, "You dated a lot before you settled down and married Alexia, right?"

Quinn chuckled. "I dated, but I didn't have a revolving bedroom door the way you do."

Cobra grinned. "Sounds like you've been listening to Cortez."

"Not just Cortez. Over the years, I've heard your mama complain about your love life as well. Your reputation is legendary. But sooner or later, that lifestyle starts to get old. Has it?"

"Let's just say I had a wake-up call when that woman tried to trap me."

"I heard about that, and no, Cortez didn't tell me. He didn't have to. He works for my firm, and I know about all my attorneys' cases."

Cobra nodded. "You know about the bet, too?"

"I heard about it. Winning will be a test of your willpower and control. But I'm sure you know that."

"Yeah, and it's hard because I've met someone."

"Recently?"

"At Colton's wedding."

Quinn nodded. "That was two months ago. So you've got three months of abstinence left, right?"

"Yes."

"I take it you don't want a steady relationship with this woman, just another short affair. One night or one week."

"What makes you think that?"

"Because it sounds like you're chomping at the bit to take her to bed, instead of using the time to establish an emotional relationship rather than a mere physical one."

Cobra thought about that. He didn't want to treat Desiree like the other women who had passed through his life. He honestly enjoyed spending time with her. "She's different, and I want to get to know her better, and I want her to get to know me."

He decided not to mention that a few weeks ago, Cortez had suggested he consider entering into a steady relationship with a woman. Considering the close call that he'd had with Bernice Whey and the fact that he'd been gun-shy ever since, maybe that was something he should consider.

"Usually, when two people take the time to get to know each other, sex is off the table in the beginning. For how long is up to the couple," Quinn said. "It's about the type of relationship you want to build, the emotional connection you want to make. But if sex is the only thing you can think about, you need to ask yourself if that's your only interest in her."

Cobra was still thinking about what Quinn had told him when he walked into his Savannah home a few hours later. He and Desiree were intensely attracted to each other; that was a certainty. In the past, that would have translated into something sexual and nothing more. So maybe there was a reason she had come into his life at a time when sex was not the main factor in the relationship.

What he told Quinn was true. He wanted to get to know her better by spending time with her. That was why he still intended to read the report from Landon that he'd received the day before he had left New York. He hadn't had the time to look at it before leaving for Savannah, but he'd make it a priority when he returned. He wasn't sure what he wanted to find. He didn't think he'd discover anything nefarious about her, but hopefully the report would help him understand her better. As much as he enjoyed being with her, there were a number of things about Allison Desiree Sharpe that didn't add up.

When Quinn was talking about Hayes and the adjustments he was making after losing both his parents, Cobra thought about Desiree. She had been placed in a similar predicament. At twelve, she had left behind friends, an aunt she had been close to, and the country where she had been born to come to live with a grandfather she barely knew. A grandfather who was going through his own grief.

Unlike Hayes, who no doubt had Quinn and Alexia, and even their kids—their daughter, Idella, and their twin sons, Blake and Bennett—to help ease Hayes into their family structure, Desiree had been shipped off to a boarding school. Not because Richard hadn't loved her or wanted her, but because emotionally, he hadn't been capable of giving her what she had needed.

But like he told Richard, the relationship between him and his granddaughter was theirs to fix, and he sincerely hoped they would.

What Cobra had to decide, however, was what type of relationship he wanted with Desiree and why. She was pulling all kinds of emotions out of him; emotions he had never felt before for a woman. Emotions he had honestly thought he was immune to. Desiree was proving him wrong.

Even now, he was missing her and couldn't wait to see her again. He wanted to show her once again that Aimery LeBlanc's claims weren't worth thinking about. Suddenly, he realized he was doing more than just priming Desiree for what was to come; he was branding her, something he had never done. He was branding her as his.

After taking a shower and slipping into bed, he decided to call Desiree. He again thought about what they had done in the Belgium Room the day before he left town. Memories of having her in his arms, of tasting and exploring her breasts with his mouth, had dominated his thoughts and made him anxious to taste other parts of her.

He punched in her phone number and waited. He felt a stirring in his stomach when she answered.

"Hello, Cobra. It's nice to hear from you. How is your family reunion going? Is everything alright?"

He settled into a comfortable position in bed. "Everything is fine. I was just thinking about you. The family reunion was a success. How did your weekend go?"

"I helped out with that reading class as usual yesterday. However, I did attend a dinner party last night that Saul and his wife gave, and I went to church with them today."

"That's great. They're a wonderful couple. Real down to earth."

"I agree, and I really like them." She paused. "When are you coming back?"

Was she missing him as much as he was missing her? "Not until Thursday. I have an early flight that morning. My brothers and I decided to stay a few days longer and hang out with the folks. They love it when the three of us are here together. And now that they have their first grandbaby and a new daughter-in-law, Mom is going all out. She is preparing all our favorite meals."

"That sounds nice." She sounded wistful.

"I'm sure it will be. Mom is the best cook in the world."

"So, what's your favorite meal?" she asked.

"Mac and cheese. She still uses her grandmother's recipe. No shortcuts or deviations."

"I bet it's delicious. I can almost feel my mouth watering now."

"It is delicious. Nobody makes it as she does. You're going to have to try it one of these days." He hadn't realized what he was insinuating until the words were out of his lips.

"Maybe I will."

At that moment, he knew that one day she would. "How about dinner Thursday night when I get back?"

"Dinner sounds nice."

"Great. At my place. Mom gave me a new recipe I want to try out."

"You cook?" she asked.

"On occasion."

"Then I'll look forward to dining with you on Thursday."

"I'll send a private car for you."

"That's not necessary, Cobra."

"It's something I want to do, so humor me."

She didn't say anything for a minute, and then gave in. "Okay."

"Good. I'll see you on Thursday around five."

"That will work. Goodbye, Cobra."

"Goodbye, Desiree."

Cobra released a deep breath. He had just done the one thing he'd sworn that he wouldn't do—invite a date to his home. The only thing that kept him sane was knowing she would not spend the night. At least not for another few months.

***

A short while after her phone call with Cobra, Desiree picked up the book she had been reading, but put it aside moments later. She couldn't get back into it. Cobra said he had called because he was thinking about her, and he had invited her to dinner at his place.

She had been thinking about him, too. A lot. After their lunch date on Wednesday, how could she not? Her breasts would never be the same. She might be imagining things, but at the sound of Cobra's voice, her nipples began to tingle mercilessly. It was as if they had recognized the voice belonging to the man who had brought them so much pleasure.

Whether she liked it or not, Cobra had gotten under her skin. And that was something, considering she'd been so fed up with selfish men that she'd decided she could do without male companionship. The last thing she had needed was to allow another one to tear down her hard-won confidence and self-esteem. For her, abstinence was one way of escaping the negative emotions Aimery had tried to make her feel.

She would always appreciate Camille, who had been there for her and offered free psychological sessions on their couch. She had refused to let Desiree blame herself for Aimery's actions. In fact, Camille had even found out what a few other people who'd been with Aimery—usually actresses—thought of his skills in the bedroom. The consensus was that he was lousy in bed. Most of them had honed their acting skills by faking their orgasms so as not to make him mad, since he was known to lavish his lovers with expensive gifts.

That revelation had made her feel better about herself, but still, she felt that abstaining for a while, giving herself time to heal, was a good idea. Aimery's words had been intentionally cruel, and for him to call another woman over to his place before Desiree could fully get dressed and leave had felt worse than any slap in the face. It had hurt her deeply. But she was over it now. Thanks to Cobra.

She couldn't believe Aimery had had the gall to show up at her office and tell her that he would have put up with her so-called 'sexual shortcomings' had he known Richard Sharpe was her grandfather. All because he wanted something from Richard. How low was that?

She regretted now that she had essentially accused Cobra of the same thing, for wanting something from her grandfather. She now knew she was wrong about that. Although she hadn't said a lot during their shared dinner that night, she'd watched her grandfather and Cobra interact with each other. They had a genuine fondness for each other. They had the kind of relationship she was just beginning to understand. Very few people gave Richard Sharpe any pushback on anything, but Cobra would disagree with him to his face.

And another thing... Cobra had pretty much destroyed Aimery's claim that she was sexually inadequate. After all, if Cobra could give her so much pleasure with just his kisses, she could barely imagine how good it would be when they finally shared a bed. And they would. She knew it in her bones.

He'd said he wanted them to get to know each other better, and she wanted that, too. But she had no idea how to turn down the heat that was already blazing out of control, between them. She wanted him and knew he wanted her. But there was that bet with his brothers keeping them apart. A bet that he was obviously determined to win.

And a part of her wanted him to win because that was what he wanted. She didn't understand the concept of sibling rivalry, but she did know she was on Cobra's side. And so she refused to do anything to hinder his chances of winning...even if it meant using her boytoy in the interim. That was something she hadn't done in years, but desperate need called for desperate measures. Her vibrator didn't come close to giving her the pleasure Cobra had, but it was better than nothing.

And he had invited her to dinner at his place on Thursday, where they would be alone. She would have to take his word that he had complete discipline over his body. She certainly hoped so, because she tended to lose all control.

When her phone rang, she recognized the ringtone she'd set for Camille. She had texted Desiree to let her know she had arrived in Zurich, but Desiree hadn't heard anything from her since. Hopefully, no news was good news.

Grabbing her phone off the nightstand, she clicked it on. "Cam? How are things going?"

"Things are going great. The cabin is nice, the Alps are beautiful, and Dre is being a perfect gentleman."

"Hmm...does that mean you haven't jumped his bones yet?"

Camille released a giggle. "No, but there have been moments when I could almost taste the chemistry between us. But he's determined to ignore it."

"Don't let him. Sometimes, you just have to go for it."

"Are you trying to give your personal therapist advice?"

She laughed. "Is it working?"

"It might be. Does this mean you and Cobra Masters have moved beyond kissing?"

"Not yet, but I know it's because of the bet he has with his brothers. But that's okay. I am willing to wait. He's a man worth waiting for, Cam."

"Sounds like Cobra has grown on you, Rae."

"If only you knew. We're still getting to know each other, but I must admit, I am enjoying the process."

"Then I am happy for you."

"Me, too. But hey, listen to this. Would you believe that Aimery is in New York, and that he came to my office?"

"What! You've got to be kidding. Why would he look you up after the way you guys ended things?"

Desiree proceeded to tell Camille everything.

"Wow, Rae. I'm so glad Cobra showed up when he did. I wonder how Aimery felt at getting told off by a real man. He is so full of himself, but there's nothing to back it up. I blame all those women who allowed him to think that he's all that."

"Well, enough about Aimery. What do you plan to do about Léandre? You've been there for almost a week."

"I know, but..."

"But nothing, Cam. If you love him—and I know you do—you have to tell him how you feel. This is the perfect opportunity."

"Yes, but now I'm getting cold feet."

"Then put on socks to warm them up."

Camille giggled again. "Okay, I will give that move some consideration."

"You'd better. I love you. I want you to be happy."

"I love you, too, Rae, and want you happy, as well."

"Hey, it's not that way with Cobra and me. We're just hot for each other. There's nothing more to it than that."

"I don't believe that. I believe there could be more between the two of you, Rae...if you let it."

"Good sex I could use, but anything beyond that is off the table."

Rather than get into an argument with her friend, Desiree said, "Listen, don't worry about me. I'm fine. I want you to concentrate on that handsome hunk that you have loved forever. You've always told me that a person is the architect of their own joy, so make yours happen, Cam. And if there are fireworks, that's even better."

CHAPTER 15

"I had fun today, Dre."

Léandre turned from the stove when Camille entered the kitchen. They had spent most of the day outside skiing and now, after getting cleaned up, they were winding down to enjoy the soup he had cooked that morning. She had stayed in her room behind closed doors a good thirty minutes longer than he had, and he figured that instead of a shower, a bubble bath in the huge whirlpool tub had been her preference.

"So did I," he said, thinking she looked good, even with her hair pulled up atop her head in one of those messy-looking buns. She had changed into a pair of loose-fitting jogging pants and a sweatshirt that advertised his production company. And she had a pair of thick socks on her feet. They were perfect for outdoors, but here, inside, with the furnace putting out a nice degree of heat, as well as the blaze in the fireplace, they seemed out of place.

"Your feet are cold?"

She looked up from where she had been reading one of the magazines on the counter. "Why do you ask?"

Was she blushing? Why? "Because you're wearing socks when it's nice and warm in here."

She shrugged. "I guess after being outside skiing all day, my feet haven't fully thawed out."

He nodded, understanding. "I've got just the thing for that. I'll give it to you after dinner. Are you ready to eat?"

"Sure," she said, closing the magazine and coming to sit down at the table.

Although the cabin had a huge dining room, he had decided after her first day that he preferred that they eat at the smaller table in the kitchen. That way, they weren't seated so far from each other that he couldn't inhale her scent. Even when they were in their teens, he'd loved the way she smelled. Especially in the evenings, after a bath.

"Need help with anything?" she asked.

"Nope, I got this. But if you'd like, you can set the table."

"I don't like, but I'll do it anyway."

He threw his head back and laughed. He'd forgotten that she had attended Mrs. Lenora's etiquette school like other kids who lived on their block. Nobody liked the lessons, but all of them learned how to deal with them. Only one person rebelled—Camille LeGraff. She'd complain that it didn't make sense for silverware to be placed a certain way, when nobody cared once they began eating. He had agreed but would never confront Mrs. Lenora about it the way Cam had. And their arguments had made those boring lessons a little easier to take.

To this day, his three older brothers adored Cam, mainly for that reason. Mrs. Lenora often spent most of their class time arguing with Camille. Before you knew it, their thirty-minute etiquette sessions were over, and they could go back outside to play.

"Hey, I'm not Mrs. Lenora. Don't complain, just do it."

"Aye, aye, sir," she said, grinning, then giving him a fake salute.

Léandre realized he had made a mistake when she entered the kitchen to get plates and silverware from the cabinets. The huge kitchen suddenly seemed small and intimate. He stared at her. Her loose-fitting jogging pants suddenly transformed into the sexiest clothing possible when she reached up to open the cabinet door, and the material stretched across her delectable-looking backside.

She turned and caught him staring. "Something's wrong?"

There was no way he would tell her that he'd been checking out her ass. "No. I was just wondering if you need my help. I'm a lot taller than you."

She frowned. "Don't rub it in. How many years have you listened to me complain about not being taller? I'm 5'6, and I always wanted to be 5'8. That was the standard height for models, and you probably remember how badly I wanted to be one."

"Of course, I remember. After all, I'm your best friend... although for the past three years, I've had to compete against Desiree."

She threw her head back and laughed, and the sound did something to him. It made every cell in his body come alive. "I can't wait to tell Desiree you said that. You sound jealous."

"I was for a while, but then I discovered I liked Desiree. Your friendship with her and your friendship with me are different. With her, it's a girl thing and with me—"

"It's a guy thing?" she interrupted to ask.

He decided not to lie. Holding her gaze for a moment, he said, "No. It's not a guy thing."

"Oh."

He saw the questioning look in her eyes, but he wasn't ready to tell her what she meant to him just yet, so he changed the subject. "Speaking of Rae, how is she adjusting to living in America?"

"She's okay. I think she's met a guy she likes."

"Already? That's fast. She's only been there a few months."

"I guess not everybody drags their feet when they see someone they want."

He nodded, accepting the rebuke. She was right. "I guess not. If she's happy, then I'm happy. I like her a lot. And not just because she's one of your best friends. She's a good person."

"She definitely is. I am blessed to have both of you in my life, Dre."

It was time to go for broke. Drawing in a deep breath, he said, "We've been friends for a long time, Cam. But I'm starting to think that's not enough. Is there another role that I could play in your life? Maybe one that brings us even closer?"

***

Camille leaned against the counter for support. He'd asked. She couldn't believe it. A few days ago, when she mentioned she was getting cold feet, Rae told her to warm them up, which was why she was wearing the socks. They were subliminal motivation, urging her to go for what she wanted.

Before dinner, she'd wondered if Dre had noticed the chemistry between them. And now, it looked like she had her answer.

Being together on the slopes had helped. He'd had to help her get reacquainted with skiing, so he'd had to touch her a lot, making sure she placed her hips and thighs in the right position as she skied, and that her equipment was sized perfectly to fit her. Each time they had touched, a little ball of need had burst to life at the pit of her stomach.

When she had walked into the kitchen to help with dinner, she'd been aware not only of his good looks, but also the stunning male power and strength he managed to radiate. She'd seen it before, but now, alone in the kitchen, it hit her hard.

"Cam?"

He was waiting for her answer, and she turned to look back at him. Even now, a crackle of energy was passing between them, hot and raw.

"I don't want to lose our friendship, Dre. And I'm so afraid I might, if I give you a truthful answer."

"That will never happen, Cam. You will always mean everything to me."

Everything? She drew in a deep breath, knowing his definition of everything might not be the same as hers. But still, since he had asked, she would answer. Holding his gaze, she said, "Yes, Dre, for years I've wanted you to play another role in my life. I've had countless dreams about it. That one day you wouldn't be just my best friend, but also my boyfriend, lover, fiancé, husband, and the father of my children. I could see us together, you working on your plays, me doing my therapy work, and the two of us raising a family. And in my dreams, we would live happily ever after...because I've loved you forever."

Releasing a deep breath, she swiped at the tears that threatened to fall. She'd put her heart out there. Would he crush her dreams? "I sound pretty pathetic, don't I?"

He slowly crossed the kitchen, walking over to her with an unreadable expression on his face, and took her hand. "You don't sound pathetic at all. Because that would make me pathetic, too."

"Pathetic, too? Why?"

He drew in a deep breath. "I have something to give you, and it's something I should have given you years ago."

Camille lifted a curious brow. "What is it?"

"Wait right here, and I'll go get it."

She watched him walk off to head in the direction of his bedroom. He returned moments later carrying what looked like a journal. This is what Kassie asked you to give me."

"A journal?" she asked, accepting it from him.

"It's more than that, Cam. Since I was in high school, I have been recording things in it. Namely, poems I would write to you."

She blinked in surprise. "You wrote me poems?"

"Yes," he said, chuckling. Quite often, in fact. Kassie discovered it under my bed when I left for college. One day she questioned me about it. That's when I admitted to her how much I loved you and had loved you forever."

She broke eye contact with him to open the book. The first poem was titled *Camille*. She silently read it and fought back tears. It was so beautiful, and knowing he had written it for her touched her deeply, making her realize the depth of his love. "You do love me, too," she said softly, amazed.

"Yes, I do love you, too, Cam. And not just as a best friend. But I was too afraid to ask for more, for the same reason you were. I didn't want to do anything to risk the close friendship we have." A smile touched his lips. "I love you, Camille Jaclyn McGraff."

Tears she couldn't hold back streamed down her face, and she couldn't swipe them away fast enough. He took the journal from her to place on the counter before leaning in to lick them away. He then pulled her into his arms and held her. The way she had always wanted to be held by him. Not as a best friend but as someone more.

He was holding her close as if he never intended to let her go. The way his body was pressed against hers made her aware of every inch of him. She was taking him all in, his scent, the heat of his skin... He pulled back slightly to gaze down at her, and the look in his eyes told her everything she needed to know. Why hadn't she taken the time to look that closely before?

"I love you, Camille. There's never been anyone but you. I read an article that said a kiss on the forehead symbolized deep love and affection, and I've kissed you on the forehead ever since."

She shook her head. "I didn't know."

"I didn't want to tell you how I felt for fear of losing our friendship. I had no idea that you had those same fears."

"Rae must have read that same article because she mentioned something about that to me. But I didn't want to get my hopes up."

"Now you know. Now *we* know. Moving forward, we will speak our feelings out loud. "I love you."

"And I love you, Dre."

Smiling, he leaned in to kiss her. And all was well with her world.

***

The moment their lips touched, Léandre was overcome with happiness. Camille loved him the way he loved her, and they would have a future together. It would be different, but they had a good base to build on. Kassie had been right all along.

The kind of kiss they were now sharing meant everything. It was what he had dreamed of for so many years. She smelled like honeysuckle, and tasted of the mint tea she enjoyed drinking every morning. Their tongues tangled, arousing him more than any kiss ever had. It felt like a welcome-home kind of kiss, and he knew immediately that that was where he was—home.

When he heard her moan, he deepened the kiss, loving the very essence of her taste and the heat of desire they were both sharing. It had taken years, but this was what was meant to be. He was putting everything he had into this, kissing her with his entire heart, body, and soul. When she moaned again, he groaned in response.

Breaking off the kiss, he pulled her into his arms, holding her close to his heart. "I love you so much, Cam," he whispered close to her ear before tracing it with his tongue. He had to say the words again, needing her to understand how much he meant them. And he would tell her every single day. He placed a feather-like kiss on her forehead, and she sighed, now knowing what it meant.

She tightened her arms around his neck and whispered. "And I love you, Dre. For always. I can't wait to read the rest of my poems."

"And you will, but not now." Sweeping her into his arms, he headed for his bedroom.

CHAPTER 16

Cobra arrived home from Savannah later than he had planned due to flight delays. Still, he had some time before his dinner with Desiree. And he couldn't wait for that. All the uncertainties and doubts he'd had about being with her had faded from his mind. All it had taken was three days spent with his brothers, who had always been his best friends. Surprisingly, they hadn't mentioned anything about the bet, and he was relieved. It was as if they had decided they'd accept the outcome, for better or worse. But then, they might not have mentioned it because they were sure they were going to win, and didn't want to rub it in. If that were the case, he would just have to prove them wrong.

After rolling his luggage into his bedroom, he pulled out the recipe his mother had given him from his carry-on bag. A short while later, he had ordered all the ingredients from the marketplace he normally used, with arrangements for everything to be delivered to his door.

He'd never invited a woman to his home for a meal. Never. But tonight, not only had he invited Desiree, but he was also actually looking forward to cooking for her.

With nothing left to do until his groceries arrived, he was about to go into the living room when he saw the packet from Landon on his dining room table. He picked it up, figuring it might be a good time to review it. Staring at it for a moment, he placed it back on the table. There was another way to handle it.

***

Desiree slid onto the leather seat of the private car Cobra had sent for her. Although she hadn't spoken with him since Sunday night, she had texted him earlier today, telling him that she was looking forward to seeing him and asking that the car pick her up from home rather than the office, so she could change clothes. She wanted to look her best for him.

She looked down at herself. She'd loved this sundress the moment she had seen it when she'd been out shopping a few weekends ago. Both excitement and apprehension were warring inside of her. She had no idea what to expect tonight.

Once she entered his home, she would be at his mercy. Well, it was too late to worry about that now. Besides, she trusted him. He had told her he had a lot of self-discipline, and he had proven it to her — several times. But there was no reason she couldn't try to tempt him and see just how far he'd go.

"We've arrived, Ms. Sharpe."

Was she here already? She remembered him telling her that he lived in Harlem, but she hadn't known his place was this close to her grandfather's home. Less than a couple of miles. Glancing out the window, she gazed at the brownstone outside the car. It was stunning, stately, and charming, just like the man who lived there.

The driver opened the car door and helped her out. She thanked him, and when she headed up the steps, the wrought-iron glass door with intricate detailing and a brushed-gold finish suddenly opened, and Cobra stepped on the stoop.

She paused so as not to miss a step. Standing there in a buttoned-up shirt and a pair of dark slacks, with his hands shoved in the pockets, he was drop-dead gorgeous. Definitely easy on the eyes.

"Hello, Desiree."

"Cobra," she acknowledged.

"Welcome to my home."

"Thanks for inviting me." Swallowing deeply, she continued up the steps.

After nodding his thanks to the driver, he reached out to assist her up the remaining two steps. Desiree felt the heat from his touch all the way to her bones, and her body trembled from the seductive look in his gaze. When they were standing directly in front of each other, close enough that if she moved even an inch, their bodies would be touching, he tightened his hold on her hand and led her into his home.

***

Cobra was nearly drowning in her scent as he escorted her inside his home. When he opened the door and saw her coming toward the steps, he had to fight back the jolt of sexual hunger that stirred to life in his midsection. She looked mouthwatering in that blue sundress with thin straps across her shoulders. The hem stopped just above her knees, showcasing a gorgeous pair of legs.

"Your home is beautiful, Cobra."

He gazed down at her. "This is the foyer. You haven't seen the rest of it. Let me give you a tour." That was something else he had never done before. Even when he lived in the condo, the only rooms his dates saw were the ones they passed on the way to the bedroom. "But first, I need this."

Lowering his head, he captured her lips, thinking that the more he kissed her, the more he needed to kiss her. She was an addiction he was starting to like a little too much. Almost as much as he loved holding her in his arms. And when she returned his kiss with as equal fervor, he wondered... What was he getting himself into?

Growling low in his throat, he reluctantly dragged his mouth away. Otherwise, he would delay giving her the tour of his home — except for his bedroom — and his brothers would win the bet. But then, why make it to his bedroom? He was very, *very* tempted to push her against the wall, unlock his zipper, pull up her dress, and push her panties aside, then slide inside of her, giving her everything he had.

"Cobra?"

At the sound of his name, he shook his head to clear it, then glanced down at her. "Yes?"

"You said something about giving me a tour."

Yes, but that was before he'd started thinking of giving her something else. "I did say that, didn't I?" Tightening his grip on her hand, he said, "Come with me, Miss Sharpe."

***

Desiree was amazed at every room they entered. The place was completely enchanting—the design of the furniture, the color scheme, the atmosphere. Every room seemed to have an identity of its own, and she loved it.

But the room that really took her breath away was his bedroom. He said the bedroom set had been handcrafted by renowned furniture maker Reese Singleton, who owned a huge warehouse in Newton Grove, North Carolina. And the double doors in the room led out to the rooftop that was almost magical.

When they returned to his living room, she sniffed the air. "Hmm, something smells good."

"I believe you will enjoy it. It's seafood spaghetti marinara. Mom and some of her friends take a cooking class in New Orleans at least once a year," he said, leading her into the dining room. "She comes back home with a couple of new recipes. When I went home the week after Colton's wedding, she tried it out on me, and I loved it. So I wanted to share it with you."

"That was a wonderful thought, Cobra. Thanks."

"Don't thank me yet. I'm just giving you a fair warning that it might not taste as good as Mom's. She has a way with food that I'm not sure I inherited. She seems to know just which spices to use to enhance the flavor. Since Dad's heart attack, she's had to curtail cooking some of her favorite dishes. They're a bit too spicy."

She nodded. "I've been meaning to tell you something, Cobra. Something I feel bad about. After you told me about your father, I realized why you're concerned about my grandfather's health, and why you got upset with me when I accused you of having ulterior motives."

Cobra brushed a lock of hair back from her face. "You accused me of something I didn't do, something I would *never* do. My friendship with Richard is solid. He's someone I admire and respect. I've learned a lot from him."

She bit back a snide comment. It wasn't Cobra's fault that her grandfather had taught him things that he hadn't bothered teaching her. "Well, I admit that I owe you an apology. I'm sorry."

"Apology accepted. And I need to apologize to you as well. I was out of line when I accused you of being jealous of me because I was here with him when you weren't. Will you accept my apology, Desiree?"

It was on the tip of her tongue to tell him that he hadn't been wrong. Maybe one day she would confess to that, but not tonight. She lowered her head. "Apology accepted."

Then, as if it was the most natural thing to do at that moment, he drew her into his arms and kissed her. She thought she would never get enough of his kisses. Each one was unique and bolder than the one before. He certainly had a way with his tongue that thrilled her, and as they kissed, her hips seemed to automatically flow into his, aligning their bodies perfectly.

As the kiss became more heated, her heart began to race, and she couldn't help but moan in feminine appreciation. He could arouse her as no man had done before. His male power surrounded her, but not to conquer her. Instead, she felt enveloped by it, embraced.

Reluctantly breaking off the kiss at the sound of her stomach growling, she licked her lips. "I guess I'm hungrier than I thought. My stomach has decided to remind me that I skipped lunch today."

"You skipped lunch? Why?"

There was no way she was telling him the thought of joining him for dinner had made her too excited to eat. Instead, she said, "I got busy. So, when do I get to try out this dish that I'm sure will taste just as good as your mom's?"

"I'm not saying it's as good as Mom's, but you get to try it out now." Still holding her hand, he led her into the dining room."

***

Cobra couldn't help grinning at the number of times Desiree told him how good the meal was. "I'm glad you enjoyed it. Mom said it makes great leftovers, and there's plenty left if you want to take some home with you."

"I'd like that. Thanks."

"You're welcome," he said, standing to start clearing off the table. She stood to help.

"You don't have to do that," he said. "I've got this."

"I don't mind helping. You fed me, and I appreciate it," she said, clearing the table as well.

Deciding not to argue, he said, "Then you can help me load the dishwasher."

It had been hard as hell sitting across the table from her and holding a conversation while so many naughty thoughts had been going through his mind. Whenever she smiled at him, a deep, primitive force tempted him to put his fork down and lean over to kiss her. Of course, he didn't. After all, he had assured her that he could control his urges. However, the restraint he'd been struggling to hold on to during dinner was slowly giving way.

Sexual tension had been a constant undercurrent between them during the meal. Even now, the air seemed to shimmer around them. Cobra shook his head. He had to get a grip; otherwise, he would be whisking her up the stairs to his bedroom. Something he swore he'd never do. Not now. Not here.

"Have you heard from Richard?" he asked, prewashing the plates, and she loaded them.

"Yes, he's texted me twice now. The last one said he's adding an additional week to his trip."

Cobra nodded. He had gotten a similar text and was glad Richard was enjoying himself with Lolita.

"You know what I think, Cobra?"

"No, what do you think?"

"He's extending his business trip because of me."

Cobra's hand went still as he gazed at her. He knew that was as far from the truth as it could get. "What makes you think that?"

She rolled her eyes. "I know you and my granddad have a close relationship, so I'm sure he's told you about my mom."

"What about her?"

"He blames her for my father's death."

"Richard has never said anything like that to me, Desiree. He told me they were out on a boat, drinking, and your mother fell overboard. Your father, who was equally drunk, jumped into the water to save her, and they both drowned. Is that not what happened?"

"Yes, that's right. But still, he blames her for forcing my dad to live that kind of lifestyle. And because I look so much like her, he indirectly blames me."

"What are you talking about, Desiree?"

***

Desiree heard the hardness in Cobra's voice and knew she had to tread lightly. After all, he was close to her grandfather and, in his eyes, Richard Sharpe could do no wrong. "My paternal grandparents never thought Mom was good enough for my dad."

"Who told you that?"

"My aunt Margot."

"What else did she tell you?"

"Mom was a party girl. She loved going out and having fun. In fact, she and my dad first met at a pub in Paris, where she often hung out. She had just finished college and was working as a journalist for Le Monde, France's leading newspaper."

She paused, thinking. "I was told that they were immediately smitten with each other and in less than three months, they ran off and got married. I remember how much they adored each other. I knew they loved me because I was a product of their love, but they also liked traveling and spending time alone together. That's how I got to spend so much time with my aunt, my mom's older sister, who was unmarried and had no kids of her own. They would leave me with Aunt Margot while they traveled all over Europe, having fun and socializing."

She took a deep breath. "According to Aunt Margot, my paternal grandparents blamed Mom when Dad started slacking at his job at the Sharpe Corporation's Paris office. They thought it was all her fault."

She saw the skepticism in his features. "I'm just telling you what I was told, Cobra."

He leaned back against the sink when she closed the dishwasher. "Even if that's true, which I seriously doubt it is, I—"

"Are you saying my aunt lied?"

"No. I'm just saying that there are two sides to every story. Even if what your aunt told you is remotely true, what does that have to do with Richard extending his trip abroad because of you?"

"I am my mother's daughter. He didn't like her, and he doesn't like me either. He only took me in because he felt he had to. After all, I was his granddaughter. But right after I came to the States, just weeks after my parents' deaths, he shipped me off to boarding school. He thinks I am my mother's clone and that I spent most of my college days partying instead of studying. And that's not true."

He crossed his arms over his chest. "Are you saying you didn't take off a semester in college to zig-zag across the country, having a good time, without letting Richard know where you were or that you were okay?"

"Yes and no."

He rolled his eyes. "It has to be one or the other, Desiree."

She gave him a frustrating look. "Yes, I took off a semester in college to zigzag across the country, but I needed that time, Cobra. My aunt had died the year before, and the day I took off was her birthday. I needed to do something to forget. I was hurting really badly," she said softly. "Aunt Margot and I always did things together on our birthdays."

She drew a deep breath. "The part about me not telling my grandfather isn't true. I called the office and left a message, asking him to call me because it was really important. I was going to tell him then what I was going through and what I planned to do about school. My first desire was to come home for a semester. When he didn't return my call—something he seldom did anyway—I assumed he couldn't be bothered. So, I took off anyway, thinking he didn't care."

"Why didn't you contact his cell phone? I'm sure you had his number."

"The boarding school I attended had a strict cell phone and social media policy. Both were banned to deter distractions. Of course, in college, things were different, but by then, Granddad had blocked my number."

"Blocked your number?"

"Yes?"

"What makes you think he did that?"

"Because whenever I called him, my phone would immediately go to voicemail. So, I got the message that he didn't want to be bothered at home, and assumed he preferred being contacted at the office."

"Are you saying he never called to check on you?"

"If he did, I wouldn't know. I wasn't allowed to have a cell phone at boarding school. In college, after I found out that he had blocked my number, I blocked his."

She paused, then shook her head slowly. "I only found out that he had been looking for me when I saw him at Colton's wedding, and he told you about that time. From what he said, I knew then that he never got my message."

"What could have happened? Who didn't give your grandfather the message?"

"His administrative assistant, Eloise Markam. In fact, I confronted her about it on my first day at the office when I was scheduled to meet with him. I told her I had recently discovered that Granddad had never received that particular message. She claimed she didn't remember me calling, but I assured her that I had called, and remembered talking to her. You should have seen how the blood drained from her face. That made me wonder how many other messages she never passed along to him, and if that's why he never returned any of my calls. Not once did she ever connect me directly to him.

She always took a message, as if she was his guard dog or something."

***

Cobra couldn't quite believe what he was hearing. He knew Desiree and Richard had issues, but damn... It sounded like those issues were deeper than he'd thought.

She honestly believed her grandfather didn't love her, and Cobra knew for a fact that was wrong. As for Richard not getting any of her messages, well, Cobra could believe that. Last year, Richard had told him that he'd had to have a serious talk with Ms. Markam after he began dating Lolita. Just like with Desiree, the administrative assistant had deliberately not passed Lolita's messages to him, giving Lolita the impression he had been avoiding her. Richard had threatened to fire his assistant if it ever happened again. If only Richard had known what the woman was putting his granddaughter through...

That was Richard's story to tell, but there was something he needed to share with her. "Come with me, will you? We need to talk about something."

She gave him a questioning look, but followed when he took her hand and led her to the living room. "What is it, Cobra?"

He sat on the sofa beside her. "We admitted tonight that we were wrong in our assumptions about each other's motives regarding Richard, right?"

"Yes."

"Well, when I wasn't sure of yours. I needed to understand why you had returned here after all this time."

"I told you. Granddad sent for me," she said

"Yes, and I believe you. But just because he summoned you, that didn't mean you had to come. I felt something wasn't right about your actions."

She frowned. "Something not right, how?"

"There was too much about you that didn't add up. I felt you had to have another motive for coming back, something other than Richard's request." He paused a moment and caught her gaze. "That hunch pushed me to order an investigation on you, to see what you were doing in Paris before you came here."

He opened the drawer under the coffee table, pulled out the packet that had been delivered last week, and placed it on the table.

***

Desiree picked up the packet, stared at it, then tossed it back on the table. She stood, her eyes blazing in anger. "How dare you have me investigated. What I did in Paris is my business. So why did you invite me over tonight? It's not like you need to find out anything. You already know everything about me—more than you have a right to know."

"That's not true, Desiree," he said, standing as well. "If you would notice, that packet is still sealed. I did not read it."

"But you planned to. Otherwise, why order it?" she snapped.

"I told you why I did it, and you're right. I had planned to read it, but I couldn't. I wanted you to be the one to tell me what's in there. It's your story, and you should tell it. I want you to be the one to share what your life was like in Paris with me."

"It's a little late for that now. Since you paid for the report, go ahead and read it for yourself. I'm leaving."

When she turned to leave, he grabbed hold of her wrist and brought her back closer to him. She glared at him. "Let go of me, Cobra. Nothing you can say or do will change my mind. Please call a car for me, or I'll call an Uber on my own. Release me!"

He let go of her wrist. "That packet will remain sealed, Desiree. I promise I won't read it. But I want you to share what's in it with me, and I can wait until you're ready. I don't want there to be any secrets between us."

She crossed her arms over her chest, and her glare deepened. "No secrets? Really? So, when were you going to tell me about the bet you made with your brothers? And that you've deliberately gotten me hot and bothered all those times, even though you never intended to take things further. You're nothing but a big tease."

A muscle jumped in his jaw. "How do you know about that bet?"

"I overheard two women talking about you in the ladies' room."

"When was this?" he snapped.

"My first day at the Sharpe Corporation," she snapped back.

He took a step toward her, anger narrowing his eyes. "And you never mentioned it."

Desiree couldn't stop the fury that spread in her stomach. "I was waiting for you to say something to me. I didn't care if you wanted to be celibate. Hell, nearly three years ago, I decided to go the celibacy route myself. I doubt that information is in your investigator's report," she lashed out.

"That's beside the point," he growled.

"For us, there is no point, Cobra." Turning, she grabbed her purse off the table and headed for the door.

Over her shoulder, she called out, "Don't bother calling for a car. I'll take a taxi home." The door then slammed shut behind her.

CHAPTER 17

Cobra stood at his office window and gazed out at the Manhattan skyline. Five days had passed since the incident with Desiree, and he didn't want to admit to missing her, but he did. He went to bed thinking about her and woke up every morning with her on his mind as well. More than once, he had reached for his phone to call her, but changed his mind. She was the one who had walked out on him—not the other way around.

Landon had warned him that the report might come back and bite him in the ass. And it had. Desiree hadn't wanted to hear anything he had to say, although he'd admitted that he hadn't read it. Well, what about her knowing about his bet with his brothers? She hadn't said anything to him about that. Nor had she admitted that she'd gone without sex for a long time too.

He turned when the buzzer on his desk sounded. He moved to it and pressed the button. "Yes, Lauren?"

"Your brother is here to see you, Mr. Masters."

He frowned. "Which one?"

"Cortez Masters."

He had spent time with his brothers last week, but Tez hadn't mentioned anything about coming to New York. "Please send him in."

He leaned against the desk as his brother walked in. "Tez, it's good to see you. I didn't know you were coming to New York," he said, after they exchanged bear hugs.

"Neither did I. It was a last-minute trip to meet with one of my clients. I just got in this morning and hope to fly out this evening. But I couldn't come to New York without checking to make sure you're okay."

Cobra frowned. "Why wouldn't I be?"

"No reason," Cortez said as he slid into the chair across from Cobra's desk. "I hope you noticed that Colt and I made a conscious effort not to say anything about the bet at the family reunion, and the days we spent with the folks afterward."

"I noticed, and it was greatly appreciated," Cobra said, sitting down in the chair behind his desk.

"We figured it would be, especially around a nosey family like ours. Very few know about that bet, and it needs to stay that way."

"Well, I hate to disappoint you, but news about it reached all the way to New York."

"How?"

"Damned if I know. The woman I'm seeing told me she knew all about it."

"You're seeing someone?"

The surprised look on Tez's face was priceless. Did his brothers think they should know every single thing he did? "Yes. But I intended to adhere to the terms of the bet while I got to know her better."

That made Tez laugh.

"And what's so funny?" Cobra asked, frowning.

"When have you ever taken the time to get to know someone better?"

That answer was easy. "Since I met Desiree."

"Desiree? Desiree Sharpe? Richard Sharpe's granddaughter?"

Cobra didn't say anything for a moment, and then nodded. "That's the one."

"Damn, man. I warned you about her after the wedding reception. Are you ready to join the unemployment line when Richard Sharpe finds out you're sniffing around his granddaughter? Do I need to remind you that he's your biggest account?"

"You don't need to remind me of anything, and I'm not sniffing around her. She and I have become friends, and after my celibacy ends, I figured we could become friends with benefits. I'm sure you remember how that works."

While Tez was attending Harvard Law School, he'd met another law student, Dahlia Fulmer, in their sophomore year. They both had big plans that didn't include getting seriously involved with anyone in the near future.

They had become good friends, and within months of meeting, had transitioned into being friends with benefits. The arrangement had worked for both of them. She was his go-to girl, and he was her go-to guy. People always assumed they were a couple, which kept other interested parties away. And because Tez and Dahlia planned to become attorneys, they'd had a lot of classes together and spent a lot of time behind closed doors, studying...and having fun between the sheets. Cobra would never forget the time he and Colton had shown up at Tez's apartment for a surprise visit...and they'd been the ones surprised.

Tez and Dahlia's friends-with-benefits relationship had lasted until their last year of law school. Then, Dahlia met someone on a summer trip with her parents to Toronto—a guy who was in medical school at Johns Hopkins. It was love at first sight, and they married within a year of graduation.

To this day, Tez and Dahlia remain friends and even exchange Christmas cards every year. According to Tez, she and her physician husband were extremely happy living in New Hampshire, with a bunch of kids.

"The situation with Dahlia and me was different," Tez said.

"How so?" Cobra asked.

"That's all we wanted to be. Friends with benefits and nothing more. That sort of relationship wouldn't work for you."

Cobra lifted a brow. "I don't see why not. Need I remind you that you're the one who suggested I stop doing one-nighters and get a steady girl?"

Cortez shrugged. "You're thinking with the wrong head, Cobra. I suggest you give this some more thought. And keep in mind that her last name is Sharpe."

"Whatever."

Tez chuckled, making Cobra study him curiously. "Your funny bone seems to be on full display today, Tez."

"I'm wondering if you truly believe all the BS you've been spouting about friends with benefits, Cobra. I know you, and I can read you like a book. You want more from Desiree Sharpe. She has gotten under your skin, pushed your buttons, and definitely ruffled your feathers. That could only mean one thing."

"What?"

You've fallen in love with her."

"Fallen in love?" Cobra asked, as if to make sure he had heard his brother correctly.

Standing, Cortez grinned. "Yes, fallen in love. It can happen, trust me, I know. And if you don't believe me, ask Colton. I just hope you figure out what you feel for her soon. A woman like Desiree won't be available for long."

Cortez glanced at his watch. "My flight takes off at six. Are you free to join me for a meal before I head to the airport?"

Cobra stood and grabbed his jacket. "I'll make time."

Because anything was better than going home to a lonely house. A house that still had Desiree's scent in every room. That was what he got for giving her that tour of his home. But he wouldn't have wanted it any other way.

But for Tez to accuse him of falling in love? That was stretching it.

At least, that was what he hoped.

***

Desiree smiled. "I am so happy for you and Léandre, Cam. You found your joy."

"Yes, I did, but don't change the subject. Let's get back to you and Cobra."

"There's nothing to get back to. And where is Léandre? Shouldn't you be somewhere curled up with him?"

"We've done a lot of curling up over the last few days, trust me, as well as a lot of other things. Dre is outdoors bringing in more wood. The temperature is going to drop tonight. It's August, but in the Alps, it feels like the middle of December."

Then, under her breath, Camille whispered, "Dre's great in bed, Rae, just like I knew he would be."

"That's too much information, Cam. If you keep it up, I'm going to have to cover my ears."

"Then let's talk about you and Cobra."

Desiree rolled her eyes as she leaned back in her office chair. "There isn't a me and Cobra. The man had me investigated for Pete's sake."

"And?"

Desiree frowned. "And? Isn't that enough?"

"He told you why. Besides, he didn't read the report."

"Then he wasted a lot of money," she quipped.

"Is there a reason you can't share with him what's in there?"

Desiree fought back tears that threatened to fall. "Yes, there's a reason. If he read it, he'd know how desperate I was to prove I wasn't like my mother...or my father, so my grandfather would love me. I wanted to show my grandfather that I was a responsible human being, worthy of my last name."

"You didn't do it for that reason, Rae. You did it for yourself. I just think you convinced yourself you were doing it for your grandfather. You were fighting for your own identity and self-worth. And you discovered both. I think you should tell Cobra, and when your grandfather returns, you should tell him, as well."

"Why should I tell Cobra anything?"

"Because I distinctly remember the last time we talked, you said that he's a man worth waiting for."

"I spoke too quickly."

"No, Rae. I think you were listening to your heart. Why don't you go ahead and admit you've fallen in love with him? I think you've both made mistakes, but there's nothing you can't work out if you really love him."

Desiree didn't say anything for a minute and then asked in a soft voice, "And if he doesn't love me back?"

"He does. If he didn't, he would have read that report the minute he got it. But he didn't. He asked you to tell him what was in it so the two of you could share it. I think that's fair."

"You would."

"Think about it, Rae. Cobra might be the best thing to ever happen to you. We already know you're the best thing to ever happen to him, and I suggest you make sure he knows it. You've always been someone who goes after what she wants, and I've always admired you for your tenacity. If you want Cobra, go and get him."

***

Hours later, Desiree was finished for the day and called Ron to pick her up. Earlier that day, she had received yet another text from her grandfather letting her know he would be extending his trip for an additional week. That was a total of five weeks now! What gives!

He didn't say why, and she had to admit, at least to herself, that the condo had been lonely without him.

She had caught the elevator down to the ground floor when she saw Cobra walking through the revolving doors. What was he doing here? Desiree paused as he walked toward her, an unreadable expression on his face. She wished her heart wasn't doing flip-flops in her chest, or that a surge of awareness wasn't trickling down her spine. More than anything, she wished she believed what Camille had told her, that she loved him...and he loved her back.

"Hello, Desiree," he said, coming to a stop in front of her.

"Cobra? What are you doing here?"

"I cancelled your ride with Ron. I wanted to be the one to pick you up."

She tightened her hand on her briefcase. "Why?"

"I'm hoping that we can talk."

"I'd like that."

She could tell from the surprise in his eyes that he had assumed she would give him some pushback

"Have you eaten yet?" he asked.

"No. What about you?"

"Tez was in town, and I shared a meal with him earlier, so I'm good."

"Well, I'm not since I missed lunch. Would you happen to have leftovers from Thursday night?"

His gaze held hers, and the way he was looking at her meant he understood the importance of her question. They both knew the leftovers were at his house, which meant he would have to take her there. "Yes, I believe I do. I'll be happy to share them with you."

"Thank you."

Taking her hand, he led her from the building.

CHAPTER 18

Cobra stepped back and let Desiree into his home. When he had walked into Sharpe Corporation and saw her again, he suddenly knew Tez had been right.

He loved her.

The impact of that realization had hit like a ton of bricks, nearly making him miss a step. And now that she was back here in his home, and she had agreed to talk, he had hope.

"I'll take your jacket." She slipped off the stylish blazer and handed it to him. Seeing the way her blouse fit over her breasts made his mouth water.

"How long will it take to thaw the pasta out?" she asked, standing before him in an oh-so-tempting beige blouse and an olive-green pencil skirt that clearly defined her curves and brought out the radiance of her hazel eyes.

He breathed in deeply, then said, "You're in luck. I took some out of the freezer this morning to eat for dinner. At the time, I hadn't known I'd be dining with Tez."

"Are you sure?" she asked. "I wouldn't want to take what could be your lunch for tomorrow."

"You won't be since I'm meeting a client for lunch." He shoved his hands in the pockets of his slacks. It was either that or give in to temptation and pull her into his arms. But he knew the worst thing he could do was assume anything and rush her. They needed to talk, so this sort of misunderstanding wouldn't happen again.

"You look nice, Desiree. But then, you always look nice."

"Thank you. So do you."

"Thanks. Come on, I'll warm up the pasta."

"Alright."

When they passed through the living room on their way to the kitchen, she paused for a moment, and he knew she had noticed the packet on the table, still in the same place she had tossed it. "Would you like a glass of wine?" he asked when they reached the kitchen.

"That would be nice."

"White or red?" he asked.

"You decide."

He nodded. "Since I cooked it with a tomato sauce, red is usually suggested. At least, that's what Mom always says."

After placing the food in the microwave, he reached into the cabinet and pulled out two wine glasses and a bottle of wine.

"And you're sure that you're not hungry, Cobra?" she asked.

He turned around and smiled. "I'm positive."

If she only knew what he truly hungered for, she might just hightail it away from the brownstone. He had spent the last five days remembering each and every moment he had spent with her, starting with Colton's wedding.

So, in a way, he should not be surprised that each time they'd been together had brought him to this moment. He had finally met a woman who could capture his heart. A woman he doubted he could live without. A woman he wanted desperately.

"I took full advantage of the fact that Cortez was paying the bill, and I ordered whatever I wanted. So, I'm not starving."

She laughed, and the throaty, sexy sound touched him deeply. He had been so sure—and so afraid—that he would never hear that laugh again. Especially not here.

The microwave dinged, and he took out the food while she poured them both glasses of wine. He actually liked this. A woman sharing space with him in his kitchen. But this wasn't just any woman. This was a woman who, without really trying, had done the impossible.

He had always figured that one day, like his brothers, he would eventually fall in love and get married. After all, his parents had been childhood sweethearts who had gotten married after college and, to this day, still loved each other deeply. His father had always said that there was a moment in every man's lifetime when he'd meet his destiny, a woman who was meant to get into his soul. And no matter what that man did, that woman would stay there, bound to him.

Of course, at the time, Cobra had assumed that his father had been speaking to Tez and Colt, since he was extremely doubtful that such a woman existed for him. And if there was someone who was meant for him, he was sure he'd be in his fifties—or even older—before he met her. Boy, he had been wrong.

After pouring the wine, Desiree followed him into the dining room. While she ate, he sipped his wine, thinking of everything he wanted to say to her. Things he had never said to a woman. But first, there was the issue of that damn investigative report between them. And that needed to be resolved.

They made small talk while she ate. She told him about a project Saul gave her to spearhead and how excited she was about it. He told her about his best friend's upcoming wedding, about how he and Sheriff Liam Strawberry had been friends since they were toddlers, and that their parents had been childhood best friends, as well. Before she left tonight, he would ask her to be his plus-one for Straw's wedding and hoped she would accept.

When Desiree finished her meal, she cleared the table and loaded her dishes into the dishwasher. Returning to the dining room, she picked up her wine glass and said, "Dinner was delicious. Thank you." She paused. "You said we need to talk. Is this a good time?"

Nodding, he stood, and after grabbing his glass and the bottle of wine, they strolled to the living room, then eased down on the sofa. They were sitting in the same place they had been the last time she'd been here, with the sealed packet in front of them.

"As you can see, I haven't read it."

She nodded. "Thank you. I want to be the one to explain my actions and the reasons I felt they were needed."

"Okay," he said, not having any idea what she was talking about.

She took a sip of wine, as if to steel herself. "When I left the States, barely a week after graduating from Rhodes, I had what I thought was a good reason. As I told you, I often felt lost and alone and needed to hear my grandfather's voice, only I couldn't get through to him. Of course, now I'm a little suspicious that he never got my messages. Still, at the time, I had no reason to think that. I assumed he was just ignoring me because he disliked my mother. And although you might think otherwise, Cobra, I still have no reason to think differently. I always made good grades in school, and even after taking off a semester in college, I still graduated on time, at the top of my class, and with honors."

"I'm sure Richard attended your graduation," Cobra said.

"Yes, he was there. And he even told me how proud he was of me, but I didn't feel it was sincere."

"Why?" he asked, reaching out and taking her hand in his. A part of him needed the connection, as well as to provide her with support.

"Mainly because Granddad is so reserved. I never know what he's feeling. He'd never given me any indication that he loved me, so why should he be proud of me for doing something I knew he had expected? It didn't add up."

She released a frustrated breath. "So I went to Paris, fully intending to act like the party girl he thought I was."

"Is that why it bothers you when people refer to you that way?"

"Yes. Because anyone who thinks that about me doesn't truly know me. If they did, they'd know how focused and driven I am."

After taking another sip of her wine, she said, "Anyway, I moved to Paris thinking I didn't care anymore and would live the life Granddad thought I was living anyway. But when I'd been there less than two months, something happened."

He lifted a brow. "What?"

A smile touched her lips. "I met Camille LeGraff. We met at a coffee shop, and immediately became the best of friends. A few months later, we moved into an apartment together."

She paused as if remembering that time. "Cam was a psychology major working on her doctorate, and I would, more times than not, be her case study." She chuckled and then added, "The sofa in our apartment is where we would hold our therapy sessions."

"That sounds interesting."

"It was. I had a lot of garbage to unload. As my unofficial therapist, she got me to see that, regardless of how my grandfather felt about me, I needed to live my life the way I wanted." She chuckled. "What's funny is that according to her, Richard Sharpe and I seemed very much alike in many ways. Cam got me to accept that being a 'party-girl' was not in my makeup, no matter what anyone thought. However, being driven to succeed was. And I discovered she was right."

"So, what did you do?"

"I enrolled in the university to work on my graduate degree. I wanted an MBA. And I didn't want to attend just any university; I wanted a degree from Harvard. Not because that's where Granddad had always wanted me to go, but because that's where I always wanted to go, too. I guess you can say that I decided to go to Rhodes College during one of my rebellious stages. I did it to spite Granddad."

"And is that why you prefer to be called Desiree? Did you see it as a way to spite Richard as well, since you believe he didn't like your mother?"

She shrugged. "I admit that was part of it, but the main reason is that being called Allison made me miss my grandmother a lot. I loved her so much."

"How did you attend Harvard while living in Paris?"

"It wasn't easy, trust me. I enrolled in the Harvard Extension School. Although the classes were online, they weren't easy. It also required that I spend so many classroom hours in Boston."

"You came to the States, and Richard didn't know?"

"I didn't want him to know. I figured he had already made up his mind about my worth. I didn't need anything to get me down, and I had to stay focused on my goal. Getting that degree was something I wanted to do to prove a point to myself. I even did my internship at the Sharpe Corporation in Paris. They had no idea I was related to the CEO."

Cobra frowned. "How could they not know you were Richard Sharpe's granddaughter?"

"I didn't tell anyone, and all my employment records are in the name of Desiree Sharpe and not Allison. So, as you can see, for almost three years I wasn't living it up in the streets of Paris, Cobra. I was working my ass off to get my MBA and learning everything I could about the company I will inherit one day."

He didn't say anything. Desiree honestly believed she was a thorn in her grandfather's side; a granddaughter he didn't care about. He hated that, but it would be up to Richard to prove otherwise. The wedge between them was bigger than he had assumed, but Cobra didn't see it as anything that couldn't be repaired. It would take effort and a willingness to meet each other halfway. But more than anything, it would take open communication.

"That's what I meant when I said that a lot about you didn't add up, Desiree. I've dated party girls, and you didn't fit the mold."

He decided he might as well go all in. "So...how did you meet Aimery LeBlanc?"

"At the theater. Camille occasionally moonlights as an actress, and to support her work, I would often go and watch her perform. Aimery and I were together for only a few months."

"Is he the reason you decided celibacy was a good idea?"

She nodded. "You heard what Aimery said that day."

"And you heard what I said, as well. It's obvious that he thinks a lot of himself," Cobra said, refilling their glasses of wine. "Men like him will shift blame every chance they get—even about their failures in the bedroom."

"It wouldn't have hurt so much if he hadn't invited another woman to come to his home to take my place before I could even leave. Not only was it hurtful, but it was also downright humiliating."

"He's a huge ass. You deserve so much better."

"There is something that I need to admit to you," she said, hesitantly.

He raised a brow. "What is it?"

She nibbled nervously on her bottom lip. "I didn't like you, even before I met you."

"Why?"

"Camille called it envious resentment syndrome. Those times when I did talk to Granddad, he would always mention you. I was jealous that you had the kind of relationship with him that I so badly wanted. He taught you how to play chess. Whenever I asked him to teach me, he would make up an excuse about not having time. So, I had to take care of it myself."

"How?"

"I joined the chess club in college and got pretty good at it. Granddad doesn't even know that I was part of Rhodes College's chess team."

"Congratulations."

"Thanks. But my jealousy of you wasn't just about chess. You had access to Richard that I never had, and every time something happened that highlighted that fact, I would get angry. The few times I did come home, he would always sing your praises, like you were the grandson he never had. And yet, there I was, the granddaughter he had…and didn't want."

Hearing the hurt in her voice, Cobra honestly didn't know what to say. Telling her that she was looking at things the wrong way would not help matters. There were just too many misunderstandings between her and Richard.

"I think you should share how you feel with your grandfather."

"And I will one day."

"I'd make it sooner than later, Desiree. That's the only way to resolve the issues between the two of you and move on. You and Richard need to talk."

"You're right. I guess in a way, it's about time." She sat back and took another sip of her wine. "So what's your story, Cobra? I've heard a lot of gossip about you, including from the women I overheard talking in the ladies' room, but I want to hear the truth from you. Why did you make a bet with your brothers that you could remain celibate for a year?"

And then leaning in closer, she added, "And I want to know what diabolical role you thought I would play in it."

CHAPTER 19

Cobra began talking, and Desiree listened. But she did more than listen. She studied his facial expressions, saw the anger in his eyes, the tightening of his jaw, and the flaring of his nostrils. Telling her about that night was not easy for him. It was making him furious all over again. The tone of his voice said it all.

When he finished, he took a sip of wine as if to wash down the memory. "And what scares me shitless is knowing that I could have lost everything that I worked so hard for, just because of one night's indiscretion, and one woman's lies. I think that's when I knew I had to do something. I've always been a one-and-done man, a guy who enjoyed the opposite sex too much to ever seriously consider settling down with one. But in one night, I discovered that the way I dealt with women could have ruined my life."

"So, it was your idea to abstain from sex for a year?" she asked.

"Not entirely. For years, my best friend Liam Strawberry, whose nickname is Straw, and who happens to be the sheriff of Savannah, would tell me that I needed to put a lock on my zipper. He felt I was getting too comfortable with the one-and-done lifestyle. Although he knew I was discerning when selecting my bed partners, he was sure that one day, some conniving woman would inevitably evade detection. And he was right. That is what happened that night. I had a lapse in judgment, and it almost destroyed everything I'd ever worked for."

He shook his head. "Both of my brothers showed up at the police station—Tez to represent me, and Colton to offer his support. Straw brought up his suggestion that I consider locking my zipper for a while, and my brothers agreed. I thought about it and decided to do it. They didn't think I could, and that's when we made a bet on whether I could remain celibate for a year. I felt it would give me time to re-strategize. Maybe come up with ways to be more careful, so nothing like what happened with that woman would ever happen again."

He looked at her. "So, that was my plan. To go without sex for a year, then return to my regular routine, only being more cautious about it. At least, that was my mindset...until I met you."

"Why me?"

"I was immediately attracted to you in a way I hadn't been to any other woman. Since I knew I couldn't sleep with you without losing the bet with my brothers, my diabolical plan, if you want to call it one, was to prime you sexually, so that when my year of celibacy ended, I would make love to you and you would want me as much as I wanted you."

She tilted her head and stared at him. "Did it ever occur to you what priming me might do to me?"

A faint smile touched his lips. "Yes, but I figured that in the end, I would have made it worth the wait for both of us. Plus, I intended to throw in a few perks along the way."

And Desiree figured no doubt he would have made it worth the wait. And those perks —that had made her experience the type of orgasms a woman only read about in romance novels – had been amazing, awesome, and kickass off the chain. Even now, the area between her legs was beginning to throb. His nearness had her senses on full alert, arousing her as no man ever had. Just the deep, sensual sound of his voice was driving her crazy.

"Of course, I had no idea you were going through a period of celibacy, as well," he added.

"Would you have done things differently had you known?"

"No. I wanted you," he said.

"Yet you denied yourself pleasure," she pointed out.

He reached up and gently stroked the side of her face. "My pleasure is seeing you get yours."

His words made a lump form in her throat, and she had to swallow a few times before she could speak. "What happened to the woman who tried to trick you? After she was arrested?"

"In the end, she got eighteen years."

"Eighteen years!"

He nodded. "And she deserved it. Let me tell you why."

She listened and felt a renewed sense of relief that Cobra had not fallen prey to the woman's schemes, as the other men had. A night spent in a stranger's bed had changed their lives forever. Hopefully, Cobra now understood that appearances could be deceiving.

She stood up, picked up the packet and handed it to him. "Considering what happened to you, I think it's a good idea for you to read it, just to verify everything I told you."

He got up as well. "There's no need for me to do that. I'd planned to shred it later."

Desiree nodded. "Well, it's up to you. Now, if we don't have anything else to discuss, I'll be going."

"I wouldn't say we didn't have anything else to talk about, Desiree," he said, reaching out to cradle the nape of her neck. "If you recall, I once told you that there are other forms of communication."

Yes, she remembered him saying that, and her nipples puckered in memory of that day when they'd shared so much more than just lunch. Just thinking about it made her feel hot, bothered, and needy. And the way he was looking at her didn't help. Nor was the placement of his hand on her neck. Her body tingled with awareness...and anticipation.

"What else do we have to talk about, Cobra?"

"I have a lot to say, Desiree." His hand moved from her neck to rest at her waist.

"Like what?" she asked in a breathy voice.

"I want to taste you again."

She swallowed deeply, and at the same time, she felt her nipples harden even more. "Taste me where? My breasts?"

"No, here," he said, easing his hand from her waist to touch her center. Mainly, the area between her legs. She could feel the heat from his hand through the material of her skirt.

The thought of what he was asking made her panties wet. Maybe now was not a good time to let him know she had never engaged in oral sex before... Then again, maybe it was. "No one has ever done that to me before. Tasted me there."

He let out a low groan as he inched his body closer to hers, and she felt his hard erection pressing against the area he had just touched. "You're kidding, right?"

Why would he think that? "No, I'm not. I've heard other women talk about it, but I've never experienced it myself. Before Aimery, there was only the guy I dated in college, but the couple of times we messed around were enough to convince me that sex was overrated."

When he continued to stare at her with something akin to disbelief in his eyes, she shrugged and added, "That one time with Aimery only confirmed what I thought."

Some might think that she was sharing too much information with him, but she didn't. She wanted Cobra to fully understand the extent of her inexperience and her disappointments. Hopefully, he now understood how much she appreciated the tender, sensual way he'd treated her. The orgasms she'd experienced with him had been her first with a man, and in her opinion, they'd been well worth the wait.

She knew the exact moment he realized what she was saying. It seemed the erection pressing against her got harder, and at the same time, his pupils darkened. "Will you let me show you how enjoyable it can be?"

Enjoyable for whom? Certainly not for him, since it was one of those pleasures where only the woman benefited. "Do you really want to, knowing you won't be getting anything out of it?"

"I told you, I get my pleasure seeing you get yours. Besides, I will be getting something out of it. I will get to know the way you taste there."

He said it as if knowing such a thing was important to him. Why? But then maybe there were some things meant for her to find out. Besides, she knew deep down that she couldn't deny him...or herself. So, releasing a deep breath, she said, "In that case, Cobra Masters, taste away."

CHAPTER 20

Cobra doubted that Desiree realized the gift she was giving him. He would be the first guy to ever go down on her, the first guy to ever know her taste there. And he deemed it an honor to show her just how miserably those other two men had failed.

A real man would make his lady's pleasure the ultimate goal. And she was his lady, although he had yet to convince her of that. But before the night ended, she'd know she was his.

Drawing her even closer to him, he took her mouth with a hunger only she could ignite within him, tangling their tongues as he reveled in her taste. This was how it was supposed to be, and how it would always be with them. He loved her, and although he did not expect her to feel the same way about him yet, he believed in his heart that one day she would.

He was one of the Masters of the Game. And now that his game had become serious, he wouldn't hesitate to use every weapon at his disposal to prove that he wanted a more meaningful relationship with her. What was between them was significant, and he intended to show her just how much. No matter how long it took. His days of avoiding commitment were over.

He broke off the kiss, filled with an urgency to taste her everywhere, especially parts of her where he had touched or tasted before. He wanted to refamiliarize himself with those areas. He'd loved how her nipples had hardened in his mouth, and this time it wouldn't only be his finger massaging her clit. He intended for his tongue to take full control.

He eased down on the sofa with her beneath him and began unbuttoning her blouse to reveal a black lace bra. He loved a woman in lace. After removing her bra, his lips tilted into a hungry smile as he savored the beauty of her breasts.

Leaning in, he captured a nipple with his mouth and began sucking hard. Her moans encouraged him to continue what he was doing, then he shifted to the other nipple. At the same time, his finger slid under her skirt to stroke her inner thigh.

"Cobra..."

He loved the way she said his name as passion escalated within her. "Yes, baby, I'm here and won't be going anywhere." *Not now or ever*, he thought.

Cobra's hand moved up her thigh, inching his fingers beneath the waistband of her panties. From the texture of the material, he could tell it was also lace, likely black, to match her bra. Inserting one finger inside of her, he found her hot and wet, just like he wanted her to be. She was ready.

Releasing her nipple, he moved back to her mouth, intending to kiss his lady senseless, until she couldn't think straight, and until she felt the world fall away.

***

Desiree truly thought Cobra was trying to drive her mad with desire. The way his mouth had taken her breasts had nearly done her in. Then, when he had slid his finger inside of her, she had to fight to stop herself from coming apart in his arms. And now he was back, making love to her mouth and scrambling her thoughts.

He broke off the kiss, leaned back, then eased down the side zipper of her skirt. "Lift up, sweetheart."

The moment she did, he slid off her skirt and tossed it to join her blouse and bra on the coffee table. "Just what I thought," he said, staring down at her. "Black lace panties."

"You don't like lace?" she asked in a ragged whisper, trying to recover from the mind-blowing kiss he had just given her.

"On the contrary, I love lace. But then, I would love cotton if you're the one wearing it."

He then slowly eased her panties down her legs, baring her entire body to his gaze. When she tried covering her middle with her hand, he said, "Don't ever be embarrassed or shy with me, Desiree. You're beautiful, and I love every inch of you."

He loved every inch of her? Surely, that hadn't been what he had meant. He probably intended to say that he liked looking at her body. But before she could give his words more thought, he wrapped her legs around his neck, lifted her hips, nudged her thighs apart, and lowered his head.

***

Oh my! Desiree felt the warm tongue penetrating her go deep, and then deeper. Holding tight to her hips, he began devouring her the same way he had taken her mouth earlier. It was as if he couldn't get enough of her. His tongue was insatiable...and she was loving every minute of it.

If he thought he was priming her for what was to come three months from now, she had news for him. She doubted she could last that long. It felt as if every inch of her sex was being sensuously invaded by his tantalizing tongue. When that same tongue suddenly touched a certain part of her, shocks of pleasure nearly stole the breath from her lungs.

Her orgasm was building, and she had a feeling he knew it, because his heated licks became even more forceful. And when what felt like a volcanic eruption started to explode inside of her, his tongue delved even deeper. She screamed his name over and over, until she was certain she didn't have any voice left. The pleasure kept coming, tearing her apart as the orgasm seemed to go on and on.

Desiree moaned deep in her chest when he gave her womanly core one long, deep lick before lowering her legs from around his neck. Then he leaned in to capture her mouth, and she could taste herself on his lips.

This orgasm had seemed more powerful than the other two combined. That said a lot about how primed she was for more...and Cobra's incredible skills in the bedroom.

For the first time ever, she felt like a true sexual being. There was no embarrassment, no shame. She wanted to own her womanhood, to take full and proud possession of it. And more than anything, she wanted to use it to satisfy Cobra. If she could give him even a fraction of the pleasure he had given her on three different occasions, then she would do her best. He'd always talk about the kind of kiss she deserved. Maybe it was time to show him what he deserved as well.

***

Cobra slowly broke off the kiss with a low, throaty groan. Not ready to release her mouth completely, he began gently sucking her lower lip, loving the sounds of the moans she made. He knew if they kept kissing, she would have swollen lips, and tomorrow was a workday for her. There was no need to give anyone in the office reason to speculate about what she was doing in her free time.

He was about to get up when she caught hold of his thighs in a firm grip. "I know you said you found pleasure in giving it to me, Cobra, but that's not good enough."

Seeing her mutinous look, he swallowed. "It's not?"

"No."

He was afraid to ask but did so anyway. "What do you have in mind?"

She hesitated for a moment, and then he watched as she took her tongue and slowly licked her lips. "I want to taste you."

His shaft began throbbing, and a rush of desire, more potent than before, rushed through his veins. "Where?"

She moistened her lip with a suggestive sweep of her tongue before using her palm to cup his already hard erection. Her touch felt hot through the material of his pants.

He opened his mouth to say that he didn't think it would be a good idea when she began lowering his zipper and easing her hand inside his boxers to ease out that part of him that was most vulnerable. The moment her hands touched his shaft, he was a goner.

She looked into his eyes. "I've never done this before, Cobra, but I want to bring you some of the pleasure you've given me. Please let me."

Then, when he didn't argue, she took him firmly in her hand and began leading his shaft toward her mouth. The mouth that he loved kissing. That same mouth he had known would one day be his downfall.

He sucked in a deep breath the moment he felt her tongue on him. Then she slowly, methodically, and deliberately began licking around as much of him as could fit into her mouth. Lord! Did she have any idea how she was making him feel? As if it had a mind of its own, his shaft began rocking against her mouth. And she, seeming determined to get as much of him as she could, licked him greedily, like she would a lollipop.

He'd managed to keep control over his reaction...until she started sucking on him hard and gripping his engorged shaft, mimicking the same rhythmic pull he'd used on her when he'd had her nipples in his mouth. It was driving him insane. He had always bragged about his self-control and discipline, but Desiree now had him in a position where he was being stripped of both.

She might have been inexperienced, but her innocent eagerness was driving him to unprecedented heights of pleasure. This was too much. *She* was too much. It felt as if every cell in his body had been electrified. When he felt himself on the verge of coming, he jerked his body back to pull himself out of her mouth. He could tell from the surprised look in her eyes that she hadn't expected that.

"What did you do that for?"

Scooping her up in his arms, he gazed down at her. "We will continue this in the bedroom."

"No, Cobra, we can't! You'll lose the bet with your brothers."

He threw his head back and laughed as he headed for the stairs. "Sweetheart, I lost the bet when you lowered my zipper and pulled out my rod."

"Oh, no! I didn't think! I'm sorry."

"I'm not. I might have lost the bet, but I gained a lot more in return. Now that you unlocked my zipper, I plan for it to stay that way. Just for you. You are the keeper of the key."

Entering his bedroom, he placed her in the middle of his bed. She was already naked, so he began removing his own clothes. "I'm not sure what you mean," she said, rising to her knees in the middle of the bed as she watched him undress.

Cobra had stripped down to his boxers. He had to make sure she fully understood. Moving toward the bed and leaning in close, he said, "You have the key...because you are the woman I love, Desiree."

She blinked. "Love?" she asked, as if she hadn't heard him right.

"Yes, love. I love you."

He hadn't expected her to break out in tears. Nor had he expected her to cry out, "I love you, too, Cobra," and throw herself into his arms.

He held her and gently stroked her back. "Why are you crying, sweetheart?"

"Because I fell in love with you and didn't think you could love me back. You've loved a lot of women."

Cobra wiped the tears from her eyes. "Correction. I loved sleeping with women. There's a difference."

"Do you still?"

"No, sweetheart. A woman called Allison brought an end to that." He shook his head, just realizing something. "How ironic is it that it was a woman named Allison who tried to ruin my life, and then another Allison — Allison Desiree Sharpe —who opened my eyes to what I truly needed in that life. One woman and only her. You are the only woman I want to sleep with. The woman who, from this day forward, holds the key to not only my zipper but also my heart."

Releasing her, he moved away from the bed and was about to dispense with his boxers when he thought of something. He looked back at her. "What about you, Desiree? Are you ready to break your celibacy project?"

She smiled. "Mine ends when yours does. I made that decision weeks ago. You are the only man I'll ever want."

Smiling, he eased his boxers down his legs and then picked up his slacks to retrieve a condom from his wallet. He knew she was watching as he sheathed himself. Then he strolled back to the bed and joined her there, immediately capturing her mouth. They had kissed numerous times before, each one more mind-drugging than the last, but this kiss was different. It was not only a kiss of commitment, trust, and mutual respect, but the main thing he was tasting in this kiss was love. Unadulterated love.

He paused and looked down at her. He wanted their gazes to be connected when he entered her. He didn't just want her to feel him; he wanted her to see love in his eyes when he moved inside her.

Holding her gaze, he slowly began to slide into her, taking his time so they could both enjoy the anticipation. Then, when he was buried deep and couldn't go any further, he smiled at her, and she returned it.

All systems were on go, and he intended to give her the ride of her life. "Ready, sweetheart?"

"Ready when you are."

He moved gently at first, then with rising passion, giving himself to her as he never had to another—completely, heart and soul. His thrusts were long and deep, and they came hard and fast. The emotions reflected in her features said she felt how special this was, too. They shared a flawless rhythm, bound together in perfect unity, totally aligned and deeply connected.

He saw the dazed look in her eyes and knew what was about to happen. "Let it go, baby. I'm right here. Right where I will always be. Let's soar through the universe together."

His words had the impact he'd intended. She released one hell of a scream and lifted her hips to receive more of his downward thrusts. He felt the intensity of their joining in every bone. Her screams urged him on, and suddenly, he felt as if he was having an out-of-body experience.

Cobra threw his head back, releasing one gigantic guttural growl as they reached orgasmic gratification together. It was only then that he collapsed beside her and held her in his arms, knowing that this was where she belonged.

***

Desiree slowly opened her eyes when Cobra returned to bed after dispensing with the condom. He drew her into his arms. "Will you go to Straw and Paula's wedding with me as my plus-one next month?"

She turned in his arms and smiled. "Of course."

He returned her smile. "And I want you to meet my parents and any other Masters who might be there."

"I will look forward to that, Cobra."

"Since I'm part of the wedding party, I have to be there early. Probably the Thursday before, since my brothers and I are in charge of the bachelor's party."

"Sounds like fun. If it's okay with you, I'll leave on the same day, and we can travel together."

He grinned. "I was hoping you would say that."

"Will you tell your brothers that you lost the bet?"

He chuckled. "I doubt if I'll have to. When they see us together at the wedding, they'll figure things out for themselves. However, I will tell my other childhood friend, Anthony Tombstone, though. It seems Tomb and Straw had their own bet going. It's only fair that I pay Tomb the two hundred dollars he will owe Straw."

He gathered her close to his arms. "I may have lost the bet, sweetheart, but I gained something far more valuable. You." He leaned in and whispered against her lips, "I love you, Desiree."

"And I love you, Cobra Masters."

CHAPTER 21

Desiree slowly opened her eyes, blinking against the bright sunlight shining through her bedroom window. She changed positions and looked up at the ceiling, realizing this was the first time she had slept in her own bed in a week. She and Cobra saw no reason to spend time apart when they didn't have to do so.

She loved waking up to him, his warm, masculine body spooning her backside. He'd make love to her the moment he realized she was awake, then, at night, they would make love and fall asleep the same way. It was like they were both making up for lost time. The only reason she had come home last night was that her grandfather had returned home.

Desiree had promised Cobra she would talk to Richard the first chance she got, though not about her relationship with Cobra, since he wanted to be the one to tell her grandfather about them. But Cobra felt she should talk to her grandfather about what Cobra thought were misconceived notions about their relationship.

She'd learned that her grandfather had no plans to go into the office until after the weekend, so she had taken the day off. There was no telling what sort of mental state she would be in after their conversation. But at least now, she had a man who loved her and who was only a phone call away.

Both she and Camille had reasons to be happy these days. Her best friend was back home in Paris and happily in love with Léandre. A wedding was planned around Valentine's Day, and of course, Desiree would be returning to Paris for that. Wild horses wouldn't keep her away. Cobra had agreed to go as her plus-one.

She smiled when her phone rang. She knew it was Cobra since she had given him his own ringtone. Picking it up off the nightstand, she said, "Good morning, Cobra."

"Good morning to you, too, love. I missed you last night."

"I missed you, too."

"I got a text from Richard. He wanted to let me know he was back and was checking to make sure our chess game is still on for tonight."

"Hmm, I'd think Granddad would want to rest up from jet lag."

Cobra chuckled. "Richard has more energy than you think. Will you be there tonight?" he asked.

"I have a special one-on-one tutoring session with one of my adult readers who couldn't make last Saturday's class."

"Where?"

"I've reserved one of the meeting rooms on the amenity floor. She works as a nanny for a family who lives in this building. It'll only take about an hour, so I'll see you before your chess game with Granddad is over."

"You will because I'm not leaving until you get home."

***

Desiree knocked on the door to her grandfather's study.

"Come in."

She entered, and her gaze immediately went to the huge window and its stunning view of the George Washington Bridge. His study was just as massive as his office at the Sharpe Corporation. Her gaze then shifted to her grandfather, who had stood when she'd entered.

"Good morning, Granddad. Welcome back."

"Thank you, Allison. Helga mentioned that you didn't go into the office today. Are you ill?"

"No, I'm fine. I took the day off because I knew you were coming home, and I wanted to talk to you about something."

He lifted a brow. "Oh? Is there something going on at the office that I need to know about?"

"No, this is personal. I hope I'm not interrupting you," she said, upon seeing all the papers spread over his desk.

"There's never a time you can't talk to me, Allison."

His words gave her pause. When she was away at school, there had never been a time when she *could* talk to him.

"Please have a seat," he said, gesturing to the chair in front of his desk.

She studied her grandfather. He looked the same, but somehow different. He seemed more relaxed, restful, and calm—not words she would usually use to describe someone who had just returned from a five-week business trip. "How was your trip?"

A smile —an actual smile —spread across his lips. "It was wonderful."

Wonderful? She could only assume the trip had been productive, and he hadn't had any issues to deal with. "I'm glad."

"So, what personal matter do you want to discuss with me?" he asked.

Desiree really didn't know how to start this conversation. But in a way, Richard had unknowingly given her the opening she needed. "I need to ask you something. Earlier, you said there was never a time when I couldn't talk to you. But if that's true, why did you block my number so I wouldn't call you when I was in college?"

Richard stared at his granddaughter, looking as if he hadn't heard her right. "I never blocked your number. Why would you think such a thing?"

"Because it's true. Of course, I couldn't use a cell phone at that boarding school in California because they were banned. But when you got me that phone just before college, I assumed you wanted me to call you now and then."

He nodded. "That was the reason I gave it to you. I don't know anything about you not being able to reach me. Why didn't you ever mention it to me when you came home for the holidays?"

She shrugged. "You were busy, and I didn't want to bother you."

"Then why didn't you call me at the office?"

"I did, several times, and I always asked that you call me back. But you never did."

He frowned. "When was this?"

"It went on for years. I called while I was in boarding school—I had to use the office phone back then. But when I was in college, I often called just because I was feeling lonely and wanted to talk to you. I missed Mom and Dad, and Gramma Allison. You were all I had left, and sometimes, I just needed to hear your voice."

***

Her words pierced his heart. Richard had always assumed that Allison had been too busy with her friends to think about calling him. But it looked as if that wasn't the case.

"I never received any messages that you called, and I certainly never got any that said you needed me to call you back. Who took your calls?"

But he already knew. The same person who had taken the messages Lolita had left, but had not passed them on to him.

"Eloise Markam. She's been your administrative assistant for years."

Evidently, too long. In fact, he had hired Eloise a couple of months before his son and daughter-in-law died, and Allison came to live with him. He stood and walked over to the window, then turned back to her. "I never received any messages that you'd called me, Allison."

"I figured as much when you mentioned that you had Landon Chestnut track me down because you thought I'd been kidnapped. I found that very odd because I'd called and left a message with Eloise, asking her to let you know I needed to talk to you. I was getting depressed and wanted to come home for a while. But when you didn't return my call, I thought you didn't want to be bothered with me, so I took off to visit places I'd never been. My friends went with me because they didn't want me traveling alone."

"I didn't know," Richard said.

"I just assumed, like the other times, you didn't care."

He left his place by the window and came to stand in front of her, leaning against his desk. "Why wouldn't I care? You're my granddaughter."

"I'm also my mother's daughter."

"What's that supposed to mean?"

She didn't say anything for a minute. Then she took a deep breath to fortify herself. It was time. "I always thought the reason you sent me to boarding school was that you didn't want me here with you, because you never liked my mom and blamed her for Dad's death. I reminded you of her, so you didn't want me around."

"You thought that?"

"Yes. Aunt Margot said you told her that you blamed Mom for Dad's death when she called to tell you about their accident."

Richard inhaled deeply. He didn't recall saying that, but hell, he could have at the time. Getting that call and being told that he'd lost his son had nearly killed him. But when he had read the police report, which included interviews with the workers on board the yacht, he realized that his son and daughter-in-law were equally responsible for their own deaths.

He saw the tears welling up in Allison's eyes, and he knew he had to try to get her to understand just what a grief-stricken mess he had been back then. "I appreciate you sharing all of this with me, Allison. And I regret that you assumed I didn't care all these years."

He paused. "Losing your grandmother was hard on me. And when I lost your father two years later, I didn't know how I'd go on. I don't recall telling your aunt that I blamed your mother, but if I did, it was during a time when my grief had become too much to bear."

He stopped talking for a moment while recalling that time. "That's not an excuse, but it's the way I felt back then.

In reality, I never blamed your mother, and I certainly didn't hold anything against you for being her daughter."

Drawing in a deep breath, he said, "The reason I sent you away to boarding school was that I was so filled with grief, and you were all that I had left. I loved you so much that the thought of losing you, too, was more than I could deal with at the time. And you were grieving for your own losses, and I was too weak to handle both mine and yours."

He rubbed his hand down his face. "But there was never a time you weren't loved or that I didn't want you."

"What about you thinking I was just like my parents, that I was a party girl who would never accept any responsibilities in life?"

"Is that something you've ever heard me say?"

"No. But I've heard others say it."

He shook his head. "Granted, that time you left school and I wasn't told, I thought it was reckless and irresponsible. Then, after reading Landon Chestnut's investigation report of how you and those other two girls were traveling from city to city, spending your time hitting one nightclub after another, it did give me that impression."

Desiree nodded. "I can see how you would think that. It had been around the time of Aunt Margot's birthday. The first one that I had to face after she was killed was hard on me. As I said, my first choice had been to come home, but when you didn't return my call, I figured you preferred that I didn't."

"As I said, I had no idea you'd tried to reach me, and I will speak with Eloise when I get back into the office on Monday. You're the second person this has happened to — where she did not pass messages on to me. But it won't happen again, I promise you that."

"Thanks for telling me that, Granddad. Because for years, I thought you didn't care for me. That's why I left here and went to Paris after college. I had to do some soul-searching. I believed you thought I was irresponsible—a party girl and no different from Mom. I went there wanting to prove you right...but couldn't."

She took a deep breath. "I ended up discovering a lot about myself in Paris. I learned that I'm not like my parents, but more like you—focused, disciplined, and ambitious. I was making something of my life."

"Would you share with me what you were doing?" he asked.

She held his gaze. "I decided I wanted my MBA, so I went back to college and got it from Harvard."

He stared at her, speechless. "You were here in the States?" he asked, shocked.

"Not the entire time." She told him about the Harvard Extension School that she attended in Paris, and the required classroom hours she had satisfied by traveling back to Massachusetts."

"I am very proud of you."

"Thanks. That means a lot." Then, she added, "There's something else you need to know."

"What?"

"I did my internship at Sharpe Corporation's Paris office. I didn't tell anyone I was your granddaughter, and I went by the name of Desiree Sharpe and not Allison Sharpe."

He couldn't stop the smile that touched his lips. "Is there anything else you've been keeping from me?"

She nodded. "When I was at Rhodes College, I was the president of the chess team. If you recall, I used to ask you to teach me, but you never had the time."

"It wasn't that, Allison."

"Then what was it?"

"I couldn't handle the memories."

She tilted her head, confused. "Memories?"

"Yes. Your grandmother and I would play chess all the time. In fact, that's how we met. We were members of the Harvard Chess Club. Chess is a game that requires full concentration, and I knew I couldn't sit across from you and not think about her. You might have inherited your mother's eyes, but you have your grandmother's smile. You favor her a lot."

Desiree gave him a cheeky grin. "She was beautiful, so I'll take that as a compliment." She paused for a moment. "I know you loved Gramma a lot. Do you ever think you will find it in your heart to fall in love again?"

"Funny you should ask."

He then told her about Lolita, that he hadn't been on a business trip for those five weeks, but had gone to visit her. And how anxious he was for Allison to meet her.

***

Now Desiree knew what was so different about her grandfather, and why he appeared so much more relaxed. "I'm really happy for you. I can't wait to meet her."

"She is looking forward to meeting you as well. She'll be back in the States in two weeks."

All this time, she'd believed her grandfather hadn't loved her. Now she knew he did, and the world suddenly seemed like a brighter place. "I'm so glad we had this talk, Granddad," she said.

"So am I, Allison. And I hope it's not the last time. You are my granddaughter, and I love you. I always have, and I always will."

He opened his arms, and she walked into them for the embrace she'd been waiting for her whole life.

***

"Checkmate," Cobra said, grinning broadly. "You're getting rusty, Richard. I won the last time we played, too. Right before you left town."

"I have a lot on my mind tonight."

"Obviously," Cobra said, leaning back in his chair. "You want to talk about it?"

Richard released a deep breath and then said. "Allison and I finally talked. You were right—it explained a lot."

"Good. I'm glad," Cobra said.

"We know it's going to be a process, but I feel so good about rebuilding our relationship. I am so proud of her."

Cobra nodded. "Rebuilding the relationship will be good for both of you. You've both been missing out on knowing each other. And you're not all that different. Now I need to ask your permission about something."

Richard lifted a brow. "What is it?"

"To marry your granddaughter."

Richard stared at him as if shocked. "Marry her? The two of you don't even get along."

Cobra smiled. "We get along just fine. In fact, we're doing some relationship-building of our own. I just wanted to make sure you are okay with it. I love her and intend to marry her."

Richard eyed him. "Marriage is a big step. I'll think about it."

Cobra chuckled. "Yes, you do that."

"Damn, Cobra. I can barely stand you as my wealth asset manager. I'm not sure if I could handle having you as a grandson-in-law."

"I'm giving you time to get used to the idea."

At that moment, they heard the door open, and Desiree came in, all smiles. Cobra was convinced each time he saw her that she was even more beautiful, and her smile would light up any room. "My two favorite guys. Who won?" she asked.

"I did," Cobra said, grinning, walking over to brush a kiss across her lips.

Desiree glanced over at her grandfather. "You let him beat you again?"

Richard shrugged. "I wasn't focused."

"Granddad, you have to uphold the Sharpe name."

"You think you can do better?" Cobra asked, grinning. "I beat one Sharpe tonight. I shouldn't have any trouble making it two."

"We'll see about that," Desiree said haughtily, placing her purse aside to sit in the chair her grandfather had just vacated.

Richard laughed. He had a feeling there would never be a dull moment with these two. And he wholeheartedly looked forward to seeing the fireworks.

CHAPTER 22

Cobra wasn't surprised when his brothers cornered him at Straw and Paula's wedding reception. "You didn't say you were bringing a date," Cortez said, crossing his arms over his chest with a smile on his face.

"Does that mean you lost the bet?" Colton asked, with an even bigger smile.

Cobra looked from one brother to the other. "Let's be clear about something. I don't think I lost anything. In fact, I gained a whole lot more. And as far as the bet goes, if straying off-course with that bet means a lifetime with Desiree, I'll proudly cash out every time."

"Straying off-course?" Colton asked, chuckling, as if amused by Cobra's choice of words.

"Yes. Desiree has a permanent key to that lock on my zipper, and I wouldn't have it any other way. So yes, Tez, you will get those airline tickets, and Colt, you'll get that trip to the Bahamas."

"Should we feel bad about collecting?" Colton asked.

Cobra grinned. "Not at all. Desiree and I will be going to her best friend's wedding in Paris in a few months, and while we're there, we're going to take a ten-day river cruise. What

I'm losing to you two is insignificant compared to a lifetime of happiness with the woman I love."

He was about to walk away when Cortez said, "Don't forget, Cobra, I called it. Being the oldest has its advantages."

Both Colton and Cobra simultaneously said, "Whatever."

"Now I have to go claim my lady for a dance," Cobra said. "I suggest the two of you find yours."

Then he walked over to where Desiree was talking to his parents and his sisters-in-law, Victoria and Kelly. He had no doubt that his brothers would not be far behind him. They never strayed far from their wives, and Cobra understood. He was happiest when he was close to his woman, too.

At that moment, he was glad the Masters triplets weren't masters of the game anymore. Now they were winners in the game of love.

***

Cobra opened the door to his home and stood aside as Desiree entered. "The wedding was beautiful, wasn't it?" she said.

He thought she looked so damn good in that dress. It showed all her delectable curves. "Yes, it was a nice wedding. I'm happy for them."

"I am, too. They're nice. In fact, everyone I met was nice. And your parents are super."

"Yes, I think I'll keep them," he grinned.

"You'd better. And have I told you how much I like your Savannah home?" she asked, glancing around.

He smiled as he closed the door and walked over to her. "I believe you have. A number of times, in fact. I'm glad you like it."

"It's so stately."

"And you, my love, are so beautiful. I love the dress you're wearing. I enjoyed watching you putting it on earlier, and I'm going to love taking it off of you now."

"You think so, do you?" she said.

"Watch me." Ignoring her shriek of laughter, he swept her into his arms and carried her up the stairs."

"You don't mess around, do you, Cobra?"

"Not when it's something I want. And I want you. It was hard to keep my hands off you at the wedding. Now I don't have to."

They entered his bedroom, and he placed her on the bed. More than ever, he was glad he had replaced the furniture in here. He'd also had Tomb permanently disconnect the video cameras. His friend had been surprised when he'd told him that he had ended the bet, but Cobra insisted he'd make it right by paying Straw the two hundred dollars Tomb would owe him. Although the security business was doing extremely well, Tomb and his wife, Erica, had four little Tombstones under the age of seven.

When Desiree began removing her shoes, he walked over to her, sat down on the bed beside her, and said, "Let me."

Placing her legs across his lap, he removed her shoes, though he couldn't resist caressing her legs. He loved the smooth feel of them. He really wanted to get her out of her dress, but he had something important to do first. He got up from the bed, then knelt in front of her.

"Cobra? What are you doing?"

He smiled as he pulled a small white box from his tuxedo jacket. Instead of answering her question, he asked one of his own. "Allison Desiree Sharpe, will you make me the happiest man alive and become my wife? I asked Richard's permission, and he said yes. I promise I will do everything in my power to make you happy."

"Oh, Cobra," she said. "Yes, I will marry you." Tears sprang to her eyes when he slid the ring on her finger.

"It's beautiful," she said, gazing at it.

She threw her arms around him. "And I promise I will do everything I can to make you happy, as well."

He believed her. Since the night they'd declared their love, his life had never been better. She made him happy. *Extremely* happy. Rising to his feet, he said. "Now to dispense with this dress."

They undressed each other in record time, and then he put on a condom. He glanced over at her, knowing she had been watching his every move. "Just so you know. Before Richard would give his permission for me to marry you, I had to agree to one thing."

Desiree lifted a brow, smiling. "Oh? And what one thing is that?"

"That we wouldn't wait too long to give him a great-grandchild."

"And you agreed to it?"

"Yes. I love kids, and I know that you do, too."

She tilted her head. "And how do you know that?"

"By your interactions with Tomb's four kids a few days ago. They didn't seem to rattle you, and by the end of the evening, they were calling you Auntie Rae Rae."

She threw her head back and laughed. "Of course they didn't rattle me. I love kids. And I can't wait to meet your nephew, Cornell. I bet he's a cutie."

"He is. Just like his Uncle Cobra."

That made her laugh even more.

"Okay, Allison Desiree Sharpe, it's time to get serious," he said, joining her on the bed and pulling her into his arms for a kiss. He had to admit that his love for her started building right after their first kiss. Nothing had changed. He was still fascinated with her mouth.

Their passion built quickly. After tasting her mouth, then pampering her breasts and her clit with his tongue, he eased into position above her.

"Do you have any more orgasms left for this?" he asked. She'd had three already.

She smiled up at him. "There are plenty more where those came from, Cobra."

He returned her smile. How lucky was he to have found a woman who took the art of multiple orgasms to an entirely new level? And to think, Aimery LeBlanc had claimed she was sexually inadequate. The guy didn't know what he'd had. But Cobra did. And he was never letting her go.

He gazed down at her, at the way her hair fanned out on his pillow, and her eyes flashed with desire. She looked like a satisfied woman who knew she was about to get satisfied yet again. Probably a few more times before they fell asleep.

Tomorrow, they would join his parents for dinner, along with his brothers and their families. He would announce their engagement then, and he couldn't wait.

"So, when do you want to get married?" he asked.

"I always wanted a June wedding."

"Then June it is, sweetheart."

He leaned in to kiss her and seal the deal, while at the same time sliding his body into hers. His lips on hers, he began moving, establishing a rhythm and setting the pace. Slow, fast, then out of control. Her body felt hot, on fire, as if it was burning for him. His thrusts were fast and hard, deliberately driving her off the edge.

Then it happened. Together, their bodies exploded in an orgasm so fierce that his head spun. He released her mouth and gazed down at her. She never looked more beautiful than when she was in her orgasmic element.

She screamed his name when another climax hit, then a third. Hell, he thought when his body began jerking again, they were headed toward a fourth. Amazing. He didn't let up until the last spasm had flowed from their bodies.

For a minute, he was too drained to speak. Somehow, he managed to ease off of her, and pulled her into his arms. "Wow," she whispered softly.

"You can say that again," he whispered back, barely breathing out the words.

She did. "Wow."

He smiled. "I love you, Desiree. Thanks for coming into my life."

She reached up and softly stroked the side of his face. "And thank you, Cobra Masters, for coming into mine."

EPILOGUE

"**I** now pronounce you husband and wife. Cobra, you may kiss your bride."

Desiree was not surprised at the thoroughness of the kiss Cobra gave her, nor was she surprised when both of his brothers, who had been his best men, tapped him on the shoulder, gesturing for him to end it.

After the minister said, "I present Cobra and Allison Desiree Masters," Cobra swept her into his arms and kissed her again as they exited the church.

The wedding reception, held at the Rockefeller Center, had been beautiful. Desiree appreciated Lolita's help in recommending the woman who had served as her daughter's wedding planner. Desiree had liked Lolita immediately and knew she was just the woman her grandfather needed. It was obvious he was happy at having a second chance at love.

Richard and Lolita would get married at the end of the year, and she was happy for them. Just before he'd walked her down the aisle, her grandfather had told her how proud he was of her. He'd said that now he had everything—the granddaughter he loved and the grandson of his heart.

The Monday after they'd had their heart-to-heart talk, he'd called Eloise Markam into his office and had given her a choice. She could resign immediately and still receive her pension, or she could be fired and receive nothing. She resigned.

The only reason she gave for her actions was that she felt she knew better than he did, what people would add stress to his life. She felt part of her job was to reduce their access to him. Desiree was glad that her grandfather had seen Eloise for the manipulative woman she was.

Desiree had never been happier in her life. And her and Cobra's wedding had been beautiful, definitely something she'd look back on with joy. She would be moving into the brownstone with him and looked forward to doing so after they returned from their honeymoon.

Camille and Léandre's wedding a few months ago in Paris had been beautiful as well. Camille had made the trip to New York to be Desiree's matron of honor. The couple had arrived a week before the wedding to take a tour of the city. They looked good together, and Camille had told Desiree about the billionaire who would be financing Léandre's next four productions.

Also, it seemed Léandre's father had finally seen the light and had decided to let his youngest son live the life he wanted. Mr. Beauchamp had also provided a nice financial backing for future productions. With her clinicals out of the way, Camille intended to open her psychology office.

Desiree glanced around the room. It would soon be time for her and Cobra to go upstairs and get dressed to leave for their honeymoon. Compliments of her grandfather, they would be spending three weeks at an exclusive resort in the Swiss Alps. She had added it to her bucket list after Camille had told her how beautiful the area was.

"Ready to begin our honeymoon?" Cobra asked.

"No."

He lifted a brow. "No?"

"No. I'm ready to begin the rest of our lives together."

As if not caring that they had an audience of over three hundred guests, he pulled her into his arms and whispered, "I love the way you think, Mrs. Masters."

He captured her mouth with his, once again reminding her that for them, it had all started with a kiss...

BRENDA JACKSON, New York Times and USA Today Bestselling author of over 150 books and novellas, and 50 million books in print, earned a Bachelor of Science degree in Business Administration from Jacksonville University. She worked in management for State Farm Insurance, where she retired after thirty-seven years. Fifty-three years ago, she married her high school sweetheart, Gerald, and they have two sons, Gerald Jr. and Brandon, ages forty-eight and forty-five, respectively. She is a member of Delta Sigma Theta Sorority, Inc.

Her professional writing career began in 1995 with the release of her first book, Tonight and Forever. Since then, she has received numerous national and literary awards and has made many trail-blazing accomplishments, which include being the first African American author to make the New York Times Bestseller's List and the USA Today's Bestseller's List in the romance genre; the Nora Roberts Lifetime Achievement Award and the Vivian Stephens Lifetime Achievement Award.

For a printable list of all Brenda's books, information on her books that were made into movies, her events scheduled, and all things Brenda Jackson, visit her website – www. brendajackson.com